Books by Alina

The Frost Brothers
    Eating Her Christmas Cookies
    Tasting Her Christmas Cookies
    Frosting Her Christmas Cookies
    Licking Her Christmas Cookies
    Resting Grinch Face

The Manhattan Svensson Brothers
    The Hate Date
    I Hate, I Bake, and I Don't Date!
    Hating and Dating Your Boss with Style!
    Yeah, I Hate-Ate Your Cupcake!
    Love, Hate, and Terrible Dates
    The Worst Dates Bring Chocolate Cake
    Dates I Love to Hate

The Richmond Brothers
    The Art of Awkward Affection
    The Art of Marrying Your Enemy

Check my website for the latest news:
http://alinajacobs.com/books.html

SLEIGH

BELLS

AND

Slaughter

A Holiday Cozy Romantic Mystery

SLEIGH BELLS AND Slaughter

ALINA JACOBS

Summary: When my high school nemesis ends up burned to death in my storage shed in the nauseatingly quaint Harrogate Christmas Market, Halloween's come early! Just because I look like Wednesday Addams's cooler, more dangerous older sister, everyone assumes I did it— including Captain Luke Reynolds, the firefighter tasked with solving the mystery of the arson and murder. Too bad my only alibi is my cat, Salem, and he's not talking.

Am I rushing into Captain Reynolds' arms to beg him to help me? Nope, I'm oiling up my brass knuckles, clearing my name, then retreating to my witchy cottage to wait out the yuletide season. But what if I end up right in the real killer's lair? All the better! Christmas needs a little spooky, and what better way than solving a murder?

*To all the witchcore
girls out there!*

With all our tricks
We're making Christmastime!

–Nightmare Before Christmas

CHAPTER 1

Lilith

I'm not sure whose idea it was to encourage people to stay in their small towns after graduation so that they can perpetuate the toxic and maladaptive relationship patterns learned in high school—including bullying, boyfriend stealing, and gossiping—but that person is even more sadistic than the one who invented that Elf on the Shelf game that drives parents insane.

I'd applaud their dedication to being evil if I weren't on the receiving end of the high-school-popularity-cesspool redux.

"Merry Christmas, Lilith!" Patty's smile was Crest-whitening-tray blinding and too wide. In her Chanel parka with matching boots, she was the picture-perfect Queen of Christmas—complete with her own entourage. Beside her, Heather and Ashley flashed equally bright and fake smiles.

Not matching their expressions, I made eye contact with each young woman. "Merry Christmas. Could I interest you in a proprietary blend of spices for your own mulled wine to celebrate the yuletide? Or perhaps a festive novelty mug, hand-painted? Maybe a clock of my own invention to count down the hours until a large man breaks into your home to eat your food and leave bags of trash—I mean presents—in your living room." I tapped the bobblehead skull on the clock. "It has a spider."

"Oh, Lilith," Patty said through gritted teeth, "you haven't changed at all since high school."

"Spooky never goes out of fashion," I replied.

"It does in December." She took in my stall in all its spooky glory. The sign that read 328 Days till Halloween. The metalwork Krampus sculpture I'd welded myself. The spider cookies artfully arranged on an antique Victorian tea tray. In a nod to the Christmas season, I'd hung mistletoe among the cobwebs, and the skulls all sported Santa hats.

Patty's nostrils flared. "I can't believe the city wouldn't let me ban your stall from the Harrogate Christmas Market. It's an eyesore, frankly."

"Won't someone think of the children?" Heather cried.

"Children love my stall," I informed her. "Even though you did make sure I have the worst spot, my stall is a viral sensation." I pointed at several girls who were filming social-media collateral in front of a mural I'd painted of Jack Skellington and Sally from *The Nightmare Before Christmas*.

"I am very much in the Christmas spirit. I even baked Christmas cookies," I said, picking up a tray. "Two for eleven dollars or one for six."

"Are those spiders?"

"In chocolate cookie form, yes."

Patty recoiled.

"You've never heard the story of the Christmas spider who sneaks into your house on the night after Christmas and removes all the regifted Christmas presents and donates them to Goodwill?" I asked, tilting my head.

Her lackeys let out little gasps.

"You're selling baked goods now?" Patty asked me, lips pursed.

"Yes, I—"

"Do you have a food permit?"

"Yeah, do you have a food permit, Lilith?" Heather and Ashley parroted at me.

"I don't need a food permit to sell cookies," I countered. "Mine are pre-bagged, and they have ribbons." I flicked one of the red bows.

"As the chair of the Christmas committee," Patty said, pulling out a red-and-gold notebook, "I am allowed to shut down stalls that are committing food-safety violations until such time as the health inspector can conduct a full, official review." She wrote furiously. "It is obvious that you are not upholding the standards of the Harrogate Christmas Market."

"*So* not upholding the standards," her fellow mean girls echoed as Patty slapped the piece of paper on the counter.

"Does she use a remote to control your reactions?" I asked dryly.

A black cat jumped onto the counter and sniffed the citation.

"Ugh, you have a cat? I'm calling animal control; that's revolting. That animal is certainly a food-safety violation," Patty continued as her mean-girl lackeys chirped.

"So gross."

"Nauseating."

Salem meowed reproachfully

"Mind your language," I told the cat.

Patty's lips curled up in disgust. "You're thirty years old. You need to grow up and stop being so weird."

"He keeps the mice away." I kicked a taxidermy rat wearing a Santa hat from his hiding spot under the lacy spiderweb tree skirt topper.

Patty screamed, clutching her notebook.

"You are a menace to this town!" she screeched at me. "You should be banned, not just from the Christmas market but from the whole town. You're a horrible influence."

"Lilith is at least trying. The skulls are all wearing Santa hats," Ashley said slowly. "David doesn't have anything Christmas related in his stall." She pointed across the narrow snow-covered pathway to a purple-and-green stall festooned with bug-eyed aliens and blurry black-and-white photos of extraterrestrial sightings.

"Shut up," Patty hissed at her. "You are not the chair of the Christmas committee. You're not even the cochair. You don't get to have an opinion."

Ashley shrank under her rage. "Sorry, Patty," she simpered.

"Christmas gestapo!" A doughy man popped up out of the alien-bedecked stall. "Lilith and I paid to be here. This isn't your Christmas market. Begone, Patty! This is why your husband can't stand you."

"You're having marriage problems?" Ashley asked in surprise, seemingly before she could stop herself.

I was shocked as well. Ricky and Patty were *the* aspirational couple in high school. Their wedding had been talked about as far away as Manhattan for how over-the-top it was.

"*Shut up, Ashley!*" Patty screamed, eyes bugging out of her head. "Ricky and I are fine! We are trying for a baby."

Heather's mouth turned down as Patty berated their friend.

"Ricky and I are very much in love, and we have the perfect life, and I'm going to have the perfect children in my perfect house in my perfect life and have perfect Christmases as soon as I shut. These. Idiots. Down."

David raced out of his stall, the buttons of his too-small *Ghostbusters* costume straining around his beer belly. "Don't try to silence me!" he yelled at Patty. "You will not shut me down!"

"As the chair of the—"

"The Christmas committee is a conspiracy! It's a scam! Lies! There is a cover-up going on in this town," he ranted, jumping in front of the girls' camera.

The teenagers screamed.

Before I could reach my broom to chase David away, Patty grabbed him, her sharp nails digging into his arm.

"You're ruining Christmas!" Patty raged. "I will have you banned from the Christmas market. You, too, Lilith. You put David up to this. You're making a mockery of me, of this town, and of this holiday."

The teenagers filmed her tirade and giggled.

"Give me that video," Patty snapped. "Heather, get it from them. It's evidence. I'm showing it to the mayor immediately."

The teen girls rolled their eyes as they sent Heather the footage.

"I'm going to file a complaint right now and have you shut down by tonight. Both of you," Patty said, snapping a photo of the citation and texting it to someone.

"She's a tyrant! Tyrant!" David bellowed after her.

"Patty, wait," I called. "You can't have me shut down. I need to sell cookies. They're my hottest item."

Patty stomped off.

After rushing to check out my customers, I grabbed the citation, stuffed it into my purse, and hurried to put on my coat. I needed to reach out to the health inspector before Patty did.

The Christmas market was crowded. Everyone in their holiday sweaters and scarves were stopped in the exact middle of the walkway, taking pictures of the quaint, picturesque town of Harrogate.

"Lilith!" a young woman called.

Like me, she was not dressed in holiday finery. My identical twin reached up a hand gloved in black lace to flick the tassel on my Christmas hat. Salem, perched on my shoulder, reached out a paw to bat her finger.

"Oh no, Sister dear, did they corrupt you too?"

"No, Morticia. However, I am about to throw Patty into a big vat of glühwein. She's having the city shut me down!" I raged. "A person can't sell cookies in the Christmas market anymore."

"We can't sell cookies?" several Christmas market vendors demanded, hurrying over to me.

"Patty's trying to get me shut down," I repeated and explained what had happened.

"Patty has too much power. She's constantly coming by and telling me I don't have enough variety in my ornament stock," a shopkeeper griped.

Another said, "Patty won't let me sell hot chocolate from a vat. Says it all has to be custom-made for each order."

"Her nonsense is cutting into my profit."

"She's trying to put me out of business," I added. "I am not going to allow it."

"Lilith, I need to talk to you," Morticia told me in a low voice. "I was just at your stall, and I—"

"Not now," I said, turning toward the historic city hall, which loomed at the end of the square. "I have to save my shop."

The bells on the city hall clock tower started clanging. Shouts of "Fire! Fire!" clashed with the ringing of the bells.

People were running in the direction of my stall, where a plume of thick black smoke curled up into the winter sky.

Salem hung on for dear life as I raced through the crush of people attracted like moths to a gas lamp at the first sign of drama.

"My stall!" I cried.

The storage shed behind it was engulfed in flames and threatening to turn my stall—*my livelihood*—into an inferno.

"Lilith, don't—"

I ignored Morticia and shoved Salem into her arms.

I made all my money during the Christmas market. Sure, my twin wouldn't let me starve on the streets, but I'd rather be burned alive than have to move in with her and her Christmas-loving boyfriend. *Blech.*

"Maybe the stupid Christmas committee could buy hoses for people!" I yelled above the roar of the fire as I grabbed the fire extinguisher and sprayed it at the scorching flames leaping out of the small window in the sidewall of the shed.

It didn't do much against the leaping flames, but it did clear them just enough for me to see inside the stall... and spot a pair of familiar Chanel boots.

"Holy Krampus!" I shouted and darted around to the front of the shed.

"Lilith!" Morticia cried, several yards away, while Salem howled and twisted in her arms. "Lilith, what are you doing? Get back!"

"I think it's Patty," I called. "I have to save her."

"It's too late. Get back."

Before I could dive for the latch on the shed door, strong arms latched around my waist.

I yelped as a firefighter, huge in his heavy gear, scooped me up and threw me into a snow drift like I weighed nothing.

Sputtering as Morticia and Salem tried to dig me out, I watched the firefighter walk into the flames and be engulfed.

People screamed.

The firefighters shouted to each other over the sound of the sirens.

"He's going to burn up! I need to save him!" I yelled, trying to fight off my sister.

But the firefighter came out of the shed, dragging a woman in soot-blackened clothes.

Motions tense, he and the other firefighters tried to work on her, but from the way they were grimly shaking their heads, I knew.

Patty was dead.

CHAPTER 2

Luke

Finally, an actual, real Yule-log-burning fire. Don't get me wrong—I don't go around wishing for tragedy, but I was a firefighter. I lived to fight fire. I was bred to fight fires.

However, during the holiday season, I'd done very little firefighting. Instead, I had been busy rescuing people who got trapped on their roofs while trying to hang Christmas lights, treating Christmas-overindulgence-induced heartburn masquerading as heart attacks, and acting as a bouncer in one of the contentious town hall meetings where everyone got tipsy on Christmas punch while the Svensson brothers railroaded whatever their latest development plan was. To be fair, the Svenssons had donated a large amount of money to restore the historic fire station in town, so I, of course, was squarely in their corner.

Now we had our first real fire of the Christmas season. As soon as the call came in, I was keyed up. Especially since this was a good fire. It wasn't someone's house or business, just a storage shed in the Christmas market.

The fire truck screeched to a halt, and I jumped out, my Dalmatian, Smokey, hot on my heels, and raced down the narrow pathway through the stalls to the burning shed, leaving the rest of the crew to unwind the hoses.

If anyone was inside, the seconds counted. And it was good I had raced over. A young woman was about to jump into the burning building. I didn't bother with niceties, just grabbed her around the waist and tossed her so I could get to work.

She sputtered and cursed from the snowdrift.

Civilians.

From the color of the flames, it wasn't a chemical fire, but with the way the fire lapped at the eaves, the shed was about to reach flashover.

"Hose! Bring the hose—"

"Watch the ice!"

"Captain, *move*!"

"Wait!" the young woman yelled above the scream of the fire engine. "Patty's in there. Save Patty."

Dammit.

Not a good fire. This was a bad fire.

Normal human beings have a primal fear of flames. Not me. There was no hesitation as I walked to the roaring flames leaping out of the small window of the storage shed. Hefting my axe, I broke down the door then twisted away as the oxygen breathed more life into the fire.

The shed reached flashover as I stepped inside the small building. I had less than a minute before it collapsed.

I hooked a woman in a white coat under her arms and dragged her out just as the first spray of water crested over me, quickly transforming into a cold deluge that engulfed the small shed.

Eddie hustled over with the medic kit. We worked on her while my dog barked and snapped, keeping the drama-hungry townspeople away.

We couldn't save her. It was clear she was gone.

Another firefighter draped a sheet over her.

"Dammit." Eddie sighed, sitting back on his heels. "Shitty way to start the season, huh?"

"Yeah." I stood up slowly, finally taking off my mask, and hooked it on my uniform. "Hell of a start."

Guilt flooded me. I should have been faster, run faster, gotten there sooner.

Mental note: schedule a fire safety session for next year. Mandatory for all persons wanting to have a stall in the market. Also, why were all the storage sheds packed so close together?

Whoever owned the burning stall had probably stuffed it full of fake snow, old wreaths, and other tinder. But why had Patty been stuck in the shed? Had she been trying to put the fire out then gotten trapped? It didn't make any sense. It was three steps into the shed. She should have been able to escape.

Or maybe someone hadn't wanted her to escape.

Smokey trotted, antsy, at my feet. He mouthed my gloved hand, trying to comfort me. I patted his black-and-white-spotted head.

Satisfied, the big dog leaped back to his job of crowd control.

Over the loudspeakers, Christmas carols played. The fire had damaged the nearby speaker, and the music was off-key. Christmas was my favorite holiday. When I got off from work, no matter how little sleep I'd had, I always walked through the Christmas market, soaking it all up—the smells, the carols, the people. Though now the Christmas market didn't feel so wholesome.

I squinted at the crowd, the spectators all in their Christmas-market finery, phone cameras up, filming to show their friends later.

One person was not in the holiday spirit.

Head to toe in black, a pale-faced young woman with dark hair falling down her back stared intently at the smoldering ruin of the shed. Her gaze slowly drifted to the body under the white sheet.

A black cat seemed to appear out of nowhere at my feet. He yowled eerily.

Smokey saw him and barked.

The cat puffed up and hissed.

The black-haired young woman walked purposefully over to me, black boots crunching in the sooty snow. She scooped up the cat then stared me down.

"Sorry for throwing you into the snowdrift," I said after a moment of that intense stare. "Do you... need medical?"

Her eyes were pools of black, her mouth a slice of dark purple turned down against pale skin as she stared at me. "No." She spun on her heel.

Chilling.

Intriguing.

She knew something.

She wasn't just mad at me for throwing her into the snowdrift. She knew something.

"All right, all right!"

Several pudgy cops jogged through the crowd toward us.

"You all can go," one of the police officers said, out of breath. Officer Bobby Browning waved to me then doubled over, hands on his knees. "The police have this under control."

The cop car was parked next to the fire truck, so it wasn't like he'd had to walk very far.

"We'll take it from here," Bobby said.

"Do you want coffee and a donut first, man?" I asked while Eddie smirked next to me.

"Fuck you."

"You missed the party, Bobby," Cliff drawled.

"I'm sure they ran here as fast as they could," Eddie said, snickering.

"Go to hell. I said we'll take it from here," Bobby huffed out.

"Don't go near that!" I bellowed as he trudged toward the shed. "It's hot."

"I know that," Bobby snapped at me as he pulled out a roll of caution tape and started stringing it up.

While I waited for the shed to cool down enough for me to investigate the source of the fire, I slowly prowled around the narrow alley where the shed was located. It was a ways away from the center of the Christmas market in the town square.

What could have started the fire? Rogue electrical wire? Was there another source of the flames?

Closing my eyes, I sniffed. If I wasn't mistaken, there was the telltale acrid scent of gasoline. But that could also be from the trucks.

Eddie had turned off the sirens. Between Smokey and the police, the crowd had begun to disperse, the harsh reality of death having sunk in. The alley was eerily quiet.

As I rounded the corner, the voices from two women were filtering out of a nearby stall. Pressing my body back against the wall, I turned my head to try to hear better.

"… you know it was Patty?"

"Yes, it was. I'm sure of it. I was just talking to her. She was going to shut down my stall."

"Hopefully her notebook burned up before she filed the citation."

"It's digital," I mouthed.

"That's not funny, Morticia."

"But it is convenient." There was something sinister in the words. Morticia was probably smiling slyly like the Grinch.

"You don't think I killed her, do you?"

"I'm just saying it's convenient."

Morticia's voice lowered. I crept closer to hear.

"… need to tell you something, Lilith," Morticia said, voice urgent.

Tell or confess?

Beside me, the black cat appeared. I held a finger up to my lips. The cat ignored it and let out a loud, curious meow and headbutted my boot.

"Salem, did you find a rat?"

Two identical dark-haired, pale-faced women peered around the corner. The only way I could tell them apart was that one of the women was wearing a very large hat held in place by hatpins decorated with bats and skulls.

"No, ma'am," I said, pushing off from the wall and entering the stall.

The twins drifted around me like ghosts of Christmas past.

"I will come find you later, Lilith," Morticia said, floating out of the stall.

Lilith clamped her mouth shut then glided over to me. "You're too big to be effective at snooping."

"I'm not snooping. I'm the captain of the Harrogate Main Fire Precinct," I said, pulling aside my heavy protective fire jacket and pointing at my badge around my neck.

"What is your business in my stall, Captain? Tarot reading? Fun holiday ornament?" She held up a ghoul wearing a Christmas vest.

"That is not a fun holiday ornament, and..." I gazed around at the Christmas or rather Halloween stall. "This is not a fun holiday stall. Did I travel through time? It looks like I'm back in October. I can't believe the Christmas committee let you get away with this, though"—I nodded to the alien stall across the path—"since this is the Christmas-market-reject corner, I suppose anything goes over here."

"I assure you this is a Christmas stall," Lilith said as I slowly prowled through the spooky wares.

"Wrong," I argued. "A Christmas stall makes you feel warm and cozy. There are painted holiday scenes, Christmas decorations, and fake snow, not fake spiderwebs."

"Christmas is a terrible holiday. I'm making it better," Lilith countered.

I stopped in front of a display with black candles and miniature gremlins riding toads wearing elf hats. "Christmas is amazing. It's about family, about being grateful for what matters."

"No, that is Thanksgiving."

"No wonder you got a citation."

"I got a citation because of pathological high school mean girl-ness. I am in the Christmas spirit. I have Christmas cookies."

She held out a tray to me.

"You're supposed to serve Santa Claus cookies. These are an abomination." I took one of the chocolate cookie spiders and bit its head off. I made an appreciative noise. "I'm a Christmas traditionalist, but these are pretty good." There was something herbal and smoky in the cookies.

"That will be six dollars." She held out her hand.

"I thought you weren't allowed to sell cookies anymore," I teased and took another bite of the spider.

The black cat meowed at me.

I held my hand out to him. "Did Mommy not make you a Christmas sweater?" The cat sniffed my fingers then headbutted my hand.

The dark-haired woman was obviously displeased. "Salem bites and scratches. Be careful."

I grinned at her and picked up the cat, who purred and rolled over in my arms. "Who's a good kitty?"

I stole another cookie off her tray. "Is this your audition for the chairwoman of the Halloween committee next year?" I asked Lilith.

"Depends. Will there be human sacrifices in the bonfire?" Her dark eyes widened as she realized what she'd said. "I mean—that's not—"

I set Salem down on the counter.

"I didn't kill Patty, Captain. I'm not a murderer."

I inclined my head to her spooky stall. "You sure about that?"

She sucked in a breath. The icy demeanor was gone, replaced by hot anger. "I know where I was, and I know what I was doing. Besides, why would I burn down my own stall to kill Patty Harrison?"

Footsteps pounded on the icy path outside the stall, then a brassy-haired young woman careened in.

"Oh my gosh, Lilith. Did you kill Patty?"

"Penny…" Lilith sighed.

I coughed.

Penny whirled around, then a smile lit up her face. "Lilith, I didn't know you had a thing for hot blonds. Guess there's a basic bitch under every goth girl."

Two splotches of color appeared on Lilith's pale cheeks. "*He is not hot.*"

I tilted my head up and grinned at her. "I am a little bit."

She slowly raised her arm and pointed with a black nail. "Out of my stall."

Figured. I finally found a girl I liked, and she was probably a murderer.

CHAPTER 3

Lilith

"People think I killed Patty Harrison?" I hissed to Penny after the fire captain had left.

"Yeah, girl!" Penny grabbed one of the spider cookies and unwrapped it.

"Why would I burn down my own stall? That doesn't make any sense."

"Keep in mind that these are the same townspeople who want the city to fund a neighborhood elf watch because they are all convinced that there is a Christmas elf infestation in the sewer and they're crawling up into people's houses to steal things."

"Your fiancé was one of the main instigators of that because it was going to distract from the big street-widening project he wants to ram through city permitting," I reminded her.

"Garrett is very much an end-justifies-the-means kinda guy. Do you have any milk?"

I made a disgusted noise and opened up the mini fridge under the sales counter.

"I have five hundred of these spider cookies. What am I going to do with them if I can't sell them?" I complained as I poured Penny her drink.

"Did the citation burn up with Patty?"

"I wish. It's all digital. Already in the system. Just got an email notification."

"Heather and Ashley are going around town bad-mouthing you, telling everyone you murdered their bestie in retaliation for her reporting your illegal activity," Penny told me.

"I am allowed to sell cookies. It's in the Christmas market bylaws."

"You can't argue that you're not suspect number one."

"Isn't the husband always suspect number one? I tried to save Patty. I need to talk to the police. This is ridiculous."

"You know the police in this town," Penny said as she dunked her cookie in the milk. "It's not like any of them were deciding between Svensson PharmaTech and the Harrogate police force. You might need to hire a private investigator or something."

"We'll see about that."

Penny and Salem followed me around the shed into the smoky winter air.

My storage shed, with all my back stock, was a pile of steaming, goopy ash. The police, as useless as always, were standing around chugging back coffee while several firefighters milled around, shouting good-natured insults at the police officers.

None of the men were even remotely doing their jobs. "Our tax dollars at work."

A large blond firefighter ducked under the caution tape to set down several boxes marked Evidence that held my more valuable and less flammable stock.

Between that and the cease-and-cookie-selling-desist order, I was going to be in the red this Christmas.

Blue eyes met mine briefly, then he turned to what was left of the shed and began scooping up little piles of ash and rubble into small glass containers and labeling them with a Sharpie.

He'd removed the heavy protective fire gear and was in tight black fire-retardant cargo pants and a black shirt with the Harrogate Fire Department logo on it.

The shirt also appeared to be the holiday cheer variation, as there were holly and snowflakes decorating the logo on the back of the shirt.

Penny grabbed my arm. "Christmas came early for you, didn't it?"

I shrugged her off. "I don't have a clue what you're going on about."

"I saw you checking out Captain Christmas." My friend waggled her eyebrows gleefully.

"*I was not.*" The words came out in a hiss of steam. "There is nothing attractive about him. He's like a dopey golden retriever, with his big, soft mouth and dumb eyes."

"Blue eyes." Penny sighed.

"Aren't you getting married soon?"

"Yes, but now you can be soon too!" She clapped her hands and jumped up and down.

"I will die single and alone with all my cats," I declared.

Salem meowed up at me reproachfully.

"She's not going to replace you, Salem." Penny bent down to pet the black cat.

Captain Christmas closed the metal box with a clang and stood up. He rolled his broad shoulders then turned toward me.

"He's coming over! He's coming over!" Penny hopped up and down next to me.

"Control yourself, Penny," I hissed.

"Ma'am," the firefighter greeted me, a smile playing around his big, dumb mouth like he knew he was hot and was just waiting for me to fall to my knees in front of him.

Not I! I have standards.

"We're all wrapped up, if you need to get back in your shed."

We regarded the smoldering ruins.

"Is this a joke? Are you serious? You're just going to leave this here?"

Captain Christmas shrugged a muscular shoulder.

"I can come back and take care of it for you," he offered. "I'm free tonight."

I stared.

Penny swooned.

He grinned.

"I don't like what you're implying, Captain."

His blond locks fell into his eyes as he dipped his head forward slightly. It was the furthest thing from sexy or alluring, of course. Also, weren't firefighters supposed to keep their hair short?

"You seriously trying to pick up a murderess, Luke?" one of the police officers called to him with a laugh. "Didn't realize you had such low standards."

I fixed a dark gaze on the officer. He withered.

"I've been in school with you since kindergarten, Winston Girthman, and I know things about you—things that could ruin you. Like what exactly you were doing in Mrs. Turner's supply closet in fifth grade."

Winston blanched.

"S-Sorry, Lilith," he stammered and backed away. "Please don't tell."

"You cannot believe I killed Patty," I said to Luke.

"I'm not ruling anything out."

"Neither am I."

"You're investigating?" His eyebrow rose.

"I am," I said, suddenly deciding.

"What a coincidence. So am I." He patted the metal case. "I'd share theories with you, but you know, everyone thinks you're a murderer."

"No!" a short and pudgy cop yelped, huffing over. "We're the police. We're the investigators. We charge people. You all put out fires. Give me that evidence."

Luke held the metal case above his head, the motion accentuating the washboard abs, bulging biceps, and ridges of muscle on his chest.

"I'll give you my report, Bobby," he said, "when it's done."

"You do that," the officer blustered.

"Uh-huh. See you around, Lilith. Hopefully not in prison." He winked.

"Who winks?" I scowled.

"Guys who look like that." Penny grabbed my arm. "Come on. I'll help you clean up."

Penny's help included dancing around the acrid remains of my livelihood and saying, "Ewww! Ew, ew, don't touch that!"

With all my wares burnt up, I really could not afford to be banned from selling cookies.

"Hold the trash bag steady," I ordered Penny.

"It's getting on my shoes," my friend complained, twisting away from my shovel. Half of the shovelful of sludgy black ash fell back to the snowy ground.

"It wouldn't if you would hold still," I reminded her.

Something glinted in the black pile at Penny's feet.

"Did you have bars of gold hidden in the shed?" she joked as I bent down to pick up the metal object. "Ew, use gloves."

I ignored my friend, twisting the metal object this way and that in the dim winter light. It was threatening to snow.

"I think it's a belt buckle," I said, "or a boot buckle."

Penny lowered her voice. "Is it Patty's?"

We regarded it.

"I'm not sure," I admitted. "It could be the murderer's and fell off when Patty was fighting for her life."

"Are you going to give it to the police?"

"Bobby managed to lock himself in the back of his patrol car at the fall festival. I have very little confidence in his ability to solve this murder."

"But they haven't even said it's murder," Penny said as I returned to cleaning up. "I mean, it could just be a tragic accident."

"Perhaps."

David, two foam aliens on his hands, danced into the alley. "Karma!" he yelled and played an air guitar. "Ding-dong, the witch is dead!"

Salem meowed.

"No offence to present company." David Reed grinned at me. It was the happiest I'd ever seen my fellow Christmas-market reject.

"Don't act so offended. I know neither of you liked Patty. She was horrible to you all in school, remember? Called you all freaks. She did it to me too. Had the whole school against us at one point. Remember how we'd have to sit by the trash cans at pep rallies?" He grinned at me. "Good times. I always thought we would end up married," he said to Penny. "You know, trauma bonding and all that. But then you wanted that billionaire, didn't you?"

My friend glared at him.

David held up his foam-covered hands. "Hey, don't sic Garrett on me. I'm just saying. Patty was horrible to all of us, and we should celebrate that she's finally gone. This is the best Christmas present ever."

"If only she had been killed before uploading Lilith's citation," Penny said.

"You didn't kill her fast enough." David clapped the foam aliens at Salem, who hissed and swiped a clawed paw.

"Maybe you could steal Patty's husband." David laughed. "Wouldn't that be the nail in the coffin?"

"I'm sure Ricky is heartbroken," I countered.

"Please." David snorted. "I bet he's at the St. Nicks martini bar tonight, celebrating his freedom. I saw the two of them fighting about something a few days ago. Patty used to manipulate him to bully me." David scowled. "Had him and his friends beat me up. I bet she turned on him too."

Hmm.

"This is a new day for Harrogate. Long live the weirdos!"

As soon as David was out of earshot, Penny leaned in. "I'd say he's suspect number one."

CHAPTER 4

Luke

The fire chief was waiting at the station when the big red truck pulled up.

"Good work out there, guys." Chief Reynolds clapped us on the shoulders as we jumped out of the truck. "I know that sometimes this job can be difficult, but I know you all tried your best to save that poor young woman."

"Poor young woman?" Cliff snorted. "Sure, whatever. Good riddance. Patty was a horrible person. She gave my sister an eating disorder."

"And the list of murder suspects just keeps climbing," I murmured.

The chief shot me a dark look. "Watch yourself, Captain."

"Aye, Chief." I gave him a two-fingered salute.

"Mayor Loring heard the sad news and sent lunch over for you all. Dig in. You need something to eat besides Christmas cookies," Chief Reynolds said.

Leaving the rest of the crew to chow down on the buffet of food, I headed back to the small room I'd turned into a lab space.

The chief followed me.

"Luke, aren't you hungry?" His eyes were full of concern. He rested a large rough palm on my shoulder.

"Can't, Uncle Don. Got a murder to investigate." I held up the metal box with the samples I'd taken at the scene of the crime.

"We don't know that's what happened." The chief sighed. "I've told you time and again, don't jump to conclusions."

When his niece, my mom, had finally lost interest in not-so-baby-cute-anymore teenage me, he took me in. It felt like he still saw me as that gangly teenager.

"Yes, I know. But I'm ninety-nine percent sure that I'm going to find accelerant, and I'm a hundred percent sure that there's a long list of murder suspects in this town."

"Or," my uncle cut in, "it could have been an accident. It's usually faulty wiring."

"Yes, I know. But I think I'm right. The police agree with me," I argued. "They're doing an autopsy report."

The chief snorted. "I ain't gonna hold my breath waiting for that one."

"Yeah, that's why I'm looking into it."

He grabbed the back of my neck. See? Still treating me like a little kid.

"Now, you listen to me, son. You listening?"

"Yes."

"Yes?"

"Yes, sir."

"You're not from this town. You didn't grow up here, and neither did I. You need to be careful about sticking your nose in where it doesn't belong. Lot of powerful people here who could make things difficult for you."

A chill traveled up my spine.

"I'm just doing my job," I reminded him.

"Just make sure that's all you're doing." He pulled me into a brief hug then released me. His salt-and-pepper mustache twitched. "I'll fix you a plate, then."

Using my shoulder, I pushed into the lab, another donation from the Svenssons.

Could they be behind the murder? They, like Cliff, had motive, I was sure. They'd grown up here, gone to school with Patty, and their wives and girlfriends had probably had run-ins with her too. Maybe as an early Christmas present, they decided to off her. Maybe that was what my uncle was trying to get at.

Nails clicked on the polished concrete floor.

Someone had given Smokey a meaty bone, and the Dalmatian pranced into the lab, tail waving, to show me his prize.

"I guess you earned it," I joked to the dog, pretending to reach for his treat.

The computer dinged as I plugged my phone in and copied over the crime scene photos. I didn't care what my uncle said. It was a crime scene. I usually had pretty good instincts when something wasn't right, first from living with a crazy mother and the crazy men she brought home, then the combat tours in the military, and now firefighting. I always trusted my instincts.

In one of the photos, a figure in black like the ghost of Christmas future hovered.

Lilith. Or maybe her twin.

They knew something, if they hadn't outright murdered Patty themselves. After all, Lilith was the one who had found the body.

After taking out the first of the samples, I began testing it for known accelerants. It didn't take long for the solvent in one of the glass vials to turn red.

"Got it," I told the dog, who was now napping off his bone. "It's definitely murder. Someone started that fire on purpose. And I need to find out who."

CHAPTER 5

Chapter 5
Lilith

It took me into the next day to clean up rest of my burnt storage shed. When I finally threw the last of the trash bags into the dumpster, all that was left was a black circle on the cobblestones.

It was dusk. Pulling up my collar, I gazed out toward the center of the town square.

Before me stretched the joyful, boisterous, colorful Christmas market. Carols streamed over the loudspeakers. It was noticeably silent in my little corner of alt-Christmas, since the speakers had been damaged in the fire and subsequently removed.

Somewhere in that Christmas cheer, a murderer lurked. It could be anyone.

Salem wound his furry body around my feet as I went back to my stall, grabbing a rag to wipe the last of the soot off my hands.

"Make any sales?" I asked the cat.

With the news of the murder and the townspeople's insistence that I'd been the perpetrator, there had been a steady stream of macabre tourist traffic to the stall. I'd spent the whole afternoon rushing back and forth, checking people out and trying to clean up behind my stall before I was slapped with yet another citation.

I'd asked Penny and Morticia if they could at least watch the stall while I cleaned. But Penny was off with her boyfriend. Morticia was off with *her* boyfriend. I was alone with my cat. Which was just how I liked it.

Right?

Right.

"I am a strong, independent woman. I do not need anyone's help."

Though it would have been nice to have a strong set of shoulders to help clean up.

Certainly not to run my nails down.

And definitely not under a Christmas-festooned T-shirt.

"You know," a teen girl said to me brightly as she brought her purchases up to the counter, "you're exactly who I want to be when I'm old—tea, tarot cards, a cool shop, an awesome cat. I'll take these two crystal skulls, please."

I stared in the mirror decorated by creepy Krampus claws after she left. "Am I old?"

"We're both in our early thirties. That means we're middle-aged. You should do a lighter makeup," Heather said to me, stepping into the stall. "Not so matte. More dewy."

Behind her, teen girls were taking photos in front of the stall. David was trying to impress people with a homemade flamethrower.

"Would be nice to have some spider cookies to sell," I muttered.

Her mouth turned down, trembling. Her eyes were red from crying, and her face was drawn and gaunt. As much as I didn't like Heather or Patty, I couldn't imagine how I'd feel if Penny had been the one to die.

"Where is it?" Heather asked meekly.

"It?"

"Where she…" Heather waved a trembling hand.

I put the kettle on to boil water for tea then led Heather out around to the back of my stall, to the site of the shed fire.

In the distance, sad Christmas tunes warbled.

Heather pressed a gloved hand to her face and let out a heartbroken sob. I patted her awkwardly on the shoulder.

"I can't believe this happened. It's like a horrible nightmare."

"Come inside." I escorted her back to my stall. "Have some tea."

I set one of the spider cookies on a plate in front of her at the small table I used for tarot card readings, added a mug of steaming water, and cast in some herbs. "Drink that."

I handed her a black lace-trimmed handkerchief.

She sipped her tea and dabbed her eyes.

"Was she…" Heather took a gulp of the hot tea. "Alive when you saw her? I just can't stand the thought of…"

"She was lying on the ground," I said carefully. "Usually with smoke inhalation, people say you go fairly quickly and painlessly."

"I don't know what I'm going to do. The Christmas committee. It just doesn't feel right without her. I don't understand who could have done such a thing. Did the police confirm it was murder?"

"Not exactly, but I could tell they all suspected it."

"Are there any suspects?" Her voice dropped to a whisper.

"You mean besides me?" I asked tartly.

Outside, several people screamed and laughed as the flamethrower roared.

Heather's eyes narrowed. "I bet it was him."

"David?"

"He's always hated Patty," Heather said darkly. "He was so angry in school when she rejected him. They used to be friends when they were kids."

"Has he been threatening her at all?" I asked carefully.

"Yesterday, and…" She was thoughtful. "He would show up at the committee offices occasionally to complain about his stall location. But then he would also ask Patty more personal questions, like how her marriage was doing."

"How is Ricky?" I asked Heather.

"He's in a state." She dabbed her eyes. "So distraught. He and Patty were the perfect couple."

"Homecoming king and queen," I said.

"And prom," Heather added primly.

Once a lackey, always a lackey.

"Nothing going on in the marriage at all?" I asked casually—or tried to.

"Ricky had nothing to do with this tragedy," Heather spat at me.

"To be fair, statistically, it's usually the husband."

"Or maybe you're trying to throw people off your trail," Heather hissed at me, standing up.

"There you are."

Ricky, a brown-haired ex-football player who'd peaked in high school, stomped into the stall. Unlike Heather, he didn't look like he'd been crying or was all that shaken up.

"Oh, Ricky." Heather practically threw herself into his arms, sobbing. "I saw where she... where she..."

Ricky patted her back awkwardly. "It's been a hard time for everyone, Heather."

He shrugged her off then grabbed the rest of the spider cookie off the plate and ate it. "We're meeting up to plan the memorial shrine in the clock tower," he told me as Heather dabbed her eyes. "Got any more of these cookies? They're really good."

"We are not bringing spider cookies to Patty's memorial."

CHAPTER 6

Luke

The security footage from the crime scene was rolling on the computer when the alarm rang late the next morning. I hadn't been able to do any more investigating the night before because we'd gotten call after call about occupancy violations at the various pop-up bars around the Christmas market.

Smokey jumped up, alert and barking.

"Not a fire," Cliff said to me as he tossed a medical bag into the truck. "Slip and fall."

Sirens blaring, the truck barreled down Main Street to the Christmas market.

"Thank you for coming so quickly." A young woman threw herself into my arms.

"Not a problem, ma'am. Where's the patient?" I asked, pulling on latex gloves.

"I'm fine," an elderly woman complained from the ground, where she was swatting at people with her enormous handbag. "Ashley, I told you I didn't need you to call 911." The elderly woman peered up at me. "Say, you were the good-looking piece of tail who put out the fire that barbequed Patty yesterday."

"Yes, ma'am," I said, bending down to gently feel her leg for any swelling or broken bones. "Does this hurt?"

"Maybe try higher."

I moved my hands up her leg.

"Higher… Higher…"

"Gran, can you please act like a normal person," the young woman hissed, "and stop harassing city employees? You're going to get us blacklisted."

"You looking for a girlfriend, sonny?" the woman asked me critically. "Too bad Noelle's taken. I have another granddaughter. She's not much to look at—three kids aren't kind to a woman. Also, she doesn't cook or clean, but she puts out, at least according to the rumors around town, and I know my son sure would like her to move out of his house."

"Thank you, but I can't date your granddaughter. That's an ethics violation," I said hastily.

"You're missing out."

"Is he, Gran?" Noelle asked.

I strangled a curse as a man threw his arm around my neck, holding his phone up and recording.

"What up! It's your boy Young Seven. I'm here with the man of the hour, Captain Reynolds, who dragged Patty's corpse outta that—"

"Sir, I am working here," I snarled.

"Yeah, and my tax dollars pay your salary," he retorted.

I stood up to my full height.

The man in front of me gulped and paled against his designer scarf.

"Fight, fight, fight!" chanted the senior citizen from the ground.

I was never going to get used to small towns.

"M-My bad, man. I'm just gonna delete that video," the streamer stammered.

"Welp, if there's no fight, I'm done here. I need to buy some hemorrhoid cream." The elderly woman used me to hoist herself to her feet while her granddaughter hovered around her.

"I'm fine, see? Fit as a fiddle." She did a little jig. "Thanks to the heroic Captain Reynolds. There must be girls lined up in front of the fire station." She cackled. "Your poor uncle's going to be beating them off with a stick."

"Yes, ma'am."

"My hero!" Ashley threw herself into my arms again, giggling as she pawed at my uniform. "I can't believe how brave you were to rush into the fire to try to save Patty."

"Just doing my job, ma'am."

She giggled. "We're the same age. I'm not a ma'am." She thrust a clipboard at me. "We're collecting signatures to designate December 12 as Patty Day."

"That's a nice way to honor your friend," I said, signing the petition.

"Isn't it?" She tugged at the bedazzled scrunchie on her wrist. "It was my idea! You know, Patty was the chair of the Christmas committee, and Heather is co-chair, but she's so upset about Patty's death that I think I'm going to have to make a motion at the next meeting that I should be chair."

The glass baubles on the scrunchie jingled as she hovered, watching me repack my medical bag. She didn't seem all that sad.

"Do you like it?" Ashley asked, holding up the scrunchie. "I made us all matching ones. I'm thinking about opening up a stall next year to sell them."

"Is that right?" I said, turning away from her.

"You know, there's a Christmas ball too. Are you coming?"

"I'm sure I'll be working that day."

"Too bad." She pouted, trailing a finger down my chest. "You shouldn't work so hard. I was thinking of having the mayor present a medal to you."

I hoisted the heavy medical bag over my shoulder.

"Did you find the murderer yet?" Ashley asked me breathlessly. "It's so horrible. Everyone thinks Lilith did it. She's always been weird. You know she used to collect roadkill and then make little skeleton decorations out of them? If anyone's a murderer, it's her."

The hairs on the back of my neck rose.

At the edges of the crowd stood a figure in black, eyes narrowed. She noticed me watching then turned abruptly.

"Wait. Lilith, wait!"

"Captain Reynolds!" Ashley cried.

I ignored her and pushed through the crowd to chase Lilith.

When I caught up to her, she was walking fast in her dark boots, which ended halfway up her calves and had lots of little black buttons, like something a Victorian ghost child would wear.

"Don't let me interrupt you," she said in a clipped tone.

"You're not. Hey!" I said, jogging to jump in front of her.

"Out of my way. I must return to my stall."

"You know, everyone thinks you did it," I told her. "Murdered Patty."

She looked up at me with those dark, almost-black eyes, like the ancient forests of Alaska at midnight on a moonless night.

"So you've told me what everyone else thinks. What do you think?"

I tugged one of her dark braids. "I think the innocent pigtail getup isn't fooling me. I think you have motive and opportunity. I think that I saw a skull in your stall that shoots flames and could have been used to start a fire. Fortunately for you, the cops are incompetent."

"Oh really? Would you arrest me if you could?" She held out her wrists, the veins dark and purple under her pale skin. "Tie me up and lock me away? Keep me as your prisoner? Be careful what you answer because I just might enjoy it. Do keep in mind that fair's fair. You lock me up, I return the favor. And I bite." She bared her teeth.

"Are you trying to intimidate me? Because it's not working," I said with a smirk. "I rush into burning buildings for fun."

"For fun." Her eyes darted away, and her eyebrows furrowed, like she'd just made a connection. "And here I thought you were in it for the paycheck."

CHAPTER 7

Lilith

"**O**h, thank god you haven't closed." Anna, the owner of the Tinsel & Tea Café, bustled into my stall. She seemed flustered and out of sorts.

"Tea?" I offered. "Cookie? Warm towelette?"

"Vodka?" Anna asked hopefully.

A flask materialized from under the cabinet. "Spiced moonshine? My own blend."

"It's got to be better than whatever they're shilling in the Christmas market." Anna removed her knitted hat.

I poured her a shot in a glass shaped like a skeleton elf holding up a stocking.

After taking a sip, Anna fanned herself and coughed. "That is strong. Is that the same spice blend that I buy for my spiced-bourbon hot chocolate?"

"Slightly different," I said, setting out the boxes of herbs used to mix the blend I'd created for Anna. I frowned. "The rest of my herbs burned in the shed. I'll have to go to my other storage unit to retrieve more for you. I'll bring this order by your shop."

"You must have ovaries of steel to still be in business with everyone in town badmouthing you and saying you're the murderer."

"I've had worse," I replied, taking out my ink and quill.

"Patty didn't make life easy for any of us." Her lips thinned. "Good thing she's dead, or she'd try to steal your hunky firefighter from you, just like she stole Ricky from me."

I spilled some of the herbs and cursed. "He's not my firefighter," I said abruptly.

"Really? Too bad. He seems nice. And hot." Anna giggled then hiccupped. "Gosh, that's strong."

"He certainly is a specimen." I made a note of the missing herbs.

"Ashley seems to think so. She's got him in her sights."

"That and the Christmas committee chair," I said, capping the bottle of ink.

"Of course she does," Anna scoffed. "Just what we need. Hopefully, someone will off Ashley too. She's obnoxious. And now they want to name a holiday after Patty? I'm going to the town hall to protest. That's an over-my-dead-body situation."

As I walked quickly through town to deliver Anna's completed order, Salem riding on my shoulder, my thoughts turned to Luke.

No, I wasn't thinking about his hair, which fell over his forehead and made him do that model-head-jerk thing to flick it out of his eyes, or the way his torso tapered to the waist with the utility belt, or the way his biceps bulged when he crossed his arms, or the lazy way he smiled at me. He was symmetrical. That was all.

No, I was thinking about how Luke had been soaking up the attention of being the small-town hero. It was suspicious. Someone had died.

Shouldn't he be in therapy or something, not parading around and letting people feel him up?

Anna's café was busy when I squeezed in. Harrogate was a mecca for people wanting to take the spirit of Christmas and inject it directly into their veins. A big part of that? The fancy, overpriced Christmas-themed drinks and food that establishments like Anna's café served.

Anna was behind the counter, piling whipped cream on her hot chocolate lattes.

Next to her? Ricky, his hand resting right above where her apron was tied around her waist.

Anna was grinning up at him. Ricky leaned down to whisper in Anna's ear, and she blushed and giggled.

Well, well, well. Ricky wasn't even trying to play the grieving husband.

Maybe he killed Patty to get back with Anna. Or maybe Patty discovered their affair.

"Lilith!" Anna waved when I approached the counter.

Ricky grabbed his order and winked at her.

What was it with men and winking? In Luke's defense, he did wink much better than Ricky did.

"Your order." I set the box on the counter.

"You're a lifesaver!" Anna took the box from me and handed me a stack of cash. "I'm going through this stuff like water, so I'll probably need another order in a few days. Hope the fire didn't dent your supply too much."

"I'll have what you need," I assured her.

What I didn't have, though, was the rest of all my metal objet d'art that I sold at my stall. The news of the murder had boosted traffic somewhat. It didn't quite make up for not being able to sell cookies. However, it was enough that I was running low on product. I needed the rest of my stock. And that was all locked up in evidence.

Time to pay the police a visit.

"I don't have it. I swear!" Winston ran around behind his desk.

"*Are you sure?*"

Salem hissed at him.

"Honest, Lilith, please don't hurt me. The fire department keeps all the fire-related evidence."

Leaving Winston to cower, I brushed past the people waiting to file complaints or pick up a drunken loved one.

The fire station was two blocks north on Main Street.

I sent a brief prayer to Hecate that Luke would be far away. Not that I was scared of him. It was just that I was having a rough week, and the last thing I needed was him spewing his holiday cheer all over my pristine black clothes.

The Harrogate fire station was lit up like one of those vintage ceramic holiday towns that people placed on their mantels. The historic building had a storybook appeal with its holiday lights and wreaths decorating the heavy brick walls.

Christmas music blared out of the open doors, and inside, men were talking.

I poked my head in.

Dammit.

Next to one of the gleaming red trucks, a makeshift gym had been set up. Luke, shirtless, was straddling one of the benches, lifting a creaking barbell loaded down with metal weights.

Not fair, I told Hecate. *I'm swapping alliances.*

The muscles under Luke's skin rippled as he pumped the heavy weights, a slight sheen of sweat on his chest. He still wore the black canvas pants and the heavy boots, ostensibly so that he could be ready to go at a moment's notice.

Ha! Ready to go.

You're so juvenile.

Luke racked the weights with a clang and sat up, his hair slightly plastered to his forehead. He swept it out of his eyes and grinned at me.

I glowered.

He laughed and made a big show of swinging his long, muscular legs over the side of the bench.

"Smokey, leave it," he scolded the dog, who was on his hind legs, whining and trying to bop Salem with his nose. "Smokey, don't get white hair all over her black clothes."

"A firefighter who named his dog Smokey. How original."

"A goth girl who named her cat Salem," he teased. "How original."

Luke grabbed his shirt from where it hung on the nearby fire truck. His abs flexed as he pulled it on.

"You know they make shirts that have more room."

"I have to pander to my adoring fans." He winked at me.

"And here I thought you got donations by sucking up to the Svenssons."

"That too." The grin broadened.

He must drink a gallon of milk a day. His teeth were perfect and white.

"Should I add you to the fan club?" he joked. "I think I might have an extra welcome packet."

"I'm not here to ogle you or stroke your already-large ego."

His bottom lip caught in his teeth at my poor choice of words. "Sure you didn't come to admire my big hose?"

My mouth twisted into a scowl. "I'm here for my shit. You all took my wares."

"Prithee tell what wares, fair lady?"

"The metal art you took from my shed. It's my property, and I want it back. The police said you have it."

"Usually, people come in here with a bribe if they want me to bend the rules for them."

"I'm already being accused of murder. I don't need extortion on that list."

"Extortion?"

Why did they make men with voices that deep?

"There're only seventeen days until Christmas. I need to be able to stock my shop. I have very little faith that you all are going to solve this murder in a timely manner," I snapped. "Especially considering you're lazing around, working out, instead of actually investigating."

"I'm waiting on a security-footage download."

"Let me see it."

Luke held out an arm to stop me. "This is official business."

I opened my oversize bag, took out a small packet, and handed it to him.

"A cookie!" His face lit up.

"A bribe."

He bit into the spider.

Beside him, his large dog slobbered.

"I don't know what you put in these cookies," he said as he led me back through the recently renovated historic firehouse to a computer room.

He clicked a few buttons on the screen, then grainy security-camera footage started playing silently. The time stamp was seventeen hours before the murder. On the screen, it was evening, the sun setting behind city hall.

"There."

A man's hooded face appeared on the screen. He was wearing dark glasses, and a scarf covered his mouth and nose as he rattled the camera then turned to look in his backpack for something. His shirt rode up, revealing the blurry hint of a tattoo.

A clue.

My eyes flicked to Luke beside me, who was intently watching the screen as the masked man, biceps bulging, aimed a can of spray paint at the camera.

"Damn," Luke said, shifting his weight.

Luke hadn't tucked in his shirt, and it rode up his back above his belt as he bent over the desk. Just below the hem of his shirt, the scrolls of a tattoo peeked out—a tattoo that looked an awful lot like the one in the video.

Ricky had tattoos too.

It would be prudent to rule out Luke, however.

I should have taken a better look when he was shirtless. Now I'd have to find some excuse to have him remove it again. Poor me.

But first, I needed to explore another hunch.

CHAPTER 8
Luke

Chapter 8

Luke

"Do you know that man?" I asked Lilith as she headed to the door.

"No," she said, "but I've seen enough."

Her behavior nagged at me.

Lilith was walking quickly out of the fire station. The way she was acting wasn't normal. Was she going to warn whoever it was? Was it her boyfriend?

"Hey, wait up!" I called after her, grabbing my coat.

Smokey grabbed his leash off the wall.

"I'm taking ten," I told Cliff, who grunted.

Jogging down the tourist-packed Main Street, I caught up with her.

"Where are you going?" I asked accusingly. "Who was that man in the security-camera footage?"

She didn't stop walking, but her head swiveled, her dark eyes piercing mine. "I told you I don't know."

"Bullshit." I matched her pace.

"I'm calling the police if you don't stop following me."

"Is that a joke?" I huffed a laugh. "Like any of those guys are going to leave their nice, warm, food-filled offices."

"I've got dirt on a number of the officers," Lilith replied.

She turned down one of the side streets off Main Street that led to one of the old Victorian neighborhoods filled with large, impeccably renovated houses.

"Don't you have to go back to work?"

"They'll call me if there's a fire. But it's all been slip and falls, health scares, boring stuff."

"Doesn't sound as exciting as a fire."

"When I quit the forest-firefighting job, I thought I would enjoy the boring life, but now I miss the excitement," I admitted.

Lilith didn't give any indication that she was listening.

Salem jumped off her shoulder and ran up the slate-slab path to the porch of a white-and-blue Victorian house impeccably decorated for Christmas with wreaths and candles in every window.

Lilith crouched next to a large hedge.

"What are—"

"Shhh!" She held up a hand.

We watched as Salem padded up and hopped onto the porch. The cat peered in the windows, sniffed at the letter slot, then meowed.

"Salem says the house is empty. Let's go."

"Your cat can't understand you," I said as we walked quickly up to the porch.

"No more than your dog understands you."

"Smokey, bark if anyone comes by," I told the Dalmatian. The dog took up his guard stance.

Lilith knelt down next to the front door and pulled out several metal lockpicks.

"Whose house is this? You can't break in. That's—"

"Done," she said, standing up and swinging the door open.

"Holy night," I whispered as I followed her inside the airy foyer. A stair draped in garland led up to the second floor. To the left was a magazine-worthy living room with a twinkling Christmas tree. On a side table were several photos of Patty and her husband.

"What are we doing in Patty's house?"

"Investigating," Lilith said in a low voice. "I'm not going down for her murder."

"What are we looking for?" I whispered as I followed her through the spacious home.

"Clues."

"About the man in the video?"

"About all suspects." She prowled into the home office. "Check in those cabinets for a life insurance policy."

"It's always the husband," I murmured.

"Correct. There's no reason why now would be any different."

Several of the drawers were filled with Christmas committee information. There were folders on various stall owners, including Lilith and David, the alien aficionado, with lists of potential violations they had committed and reasons to ban them.

I snapped a few photos as I flipped through the contents of the folder. "This woman made a lot of enemies."

"I'm sure the list of who didn't want her dead is going to be the easier one to populate," Lilith agreed as she rifled through drawers.

Lilith suddenly appeared next to me. She smelled like some sort of herbal spice, a little like Christmas trees and faintly sweet. It was intoxicating, like her cookies.

"Found the life insurance policy." She set a folder on the desk. "Ricky is set to receive two million dollars."

I whistled.

"Find anything?" she asked me, sifting through the papers on the desk.

"Patty has more folders on people than the Stasi."

"Take a look at this." Lilith held up the notepad to me.

"It's a blank pad."

"But Patty had been writing something on it. Do you ever visit forgotten graveyards?" she asked.

Out of her pocket came a piece of charcoal. It scraped against the paper as she carefully rubbed over it to reveal the imprint of the last note Patty had written before she died.

Life has its secrets, and I've unearthed one of yours. No one in this town knows you were adopted. Except me. If you want your true roots to remain hidden, you'll have to make it worth my while. Or watch your life unravel before your eyes. The choice is yours.

"Does it have a name?" I asked Lilith.

"No." She carefully folded up the charcoal paper and slipped it into her bag.

"Maybe Ricky wrote it," I suggested as she headed upstairs.

"No, that's Patty's handwriting. If we find out who she was blackmailing, we find the killer."

CHAPTER 9

Lilith

A multitude of clues, all of them pointing in opposite directions, was leading me no closer to the murderer or to clearing my name.

"It must be someone Patty hated to blackmail like that," Luke said with a frown.

"Not necessarily." I threw open the doors to the master suite. "Patty enjoyed psychologically tormenting people."

As impeccably turned out as the rest of the house, the master suite was decorated like a fancy hotel room. Toward the back of the high-ceilinged room was the bed, littered with fancy throw pillows. In one corner was a reading nook, with a bookshelf that held a number of Ricky's high school football trophies. An armchair with a Christmas-themed throw was nestled next to the bookshelves.

I headed to the closet to see if I could find a match for the belt buckle. Luke wandered to the bookshelf.

Satisfied he was occupied, I quickly scanned Patty's boots. She only wore designer, and all of her high-fashion clothing items had the name of a fashion house prominently displayed on every button, clasp, and buckle. There wasn't anything similar in her accessories, just a number of scrunchies, brooches, and a lot of jewelry. Her Christmas accessories were front and center. For someone who spent a lot of money on her clothes, they sure were gaudy. Nothing like the buckle I'd found, which was plain and masculine. And definitely not Patty's.

I turned to Ricky's side of the closet. His boots, coats, and ski gear all seemed to have their buckles, and the one I had didn't match any of them.

Another dead end.

I wasn't crossing Ricky off my list yet. But I'd have to pursue other clues, like the blackmail letter. Patty was a mean girl through and through. She had not left that behavior behind in high school.

I flicked off the closet light and headed back into the master suite. "I'm done. Let's go."

"Aw," Luke said, flipping through a yearbook. "Wait, let's find Lilith from high school."

"A tome of the worst years of my life. Glad you find it amusing."

"Look at mini Lilith!" He held up a spread of colorful photos. Patty had drawn horns on my headshot. "Not smiling?" he asked, studying my photo.

I peered at it. "Actually, I look very happy in that photo. It was senior year, and I was counting down the months until I was free."

He flipped through more pages of the yearbook. "Patty and Ricky sure were popular," he remarked.

"They feature in every photo because Patty told Heather to be the yearbook editor and make sure she had top billing," I explained.

"Poor Heather. She lost her whole reason for being."

Next to one of the photos of Ricky posing dramatically with the state high school football championship trophy, Patty had written, *My one and only true love!* with lots of hearts around him.

"If I find your yearbook, will it also have hearts and flowers drawn around Ricky?" Luke grinned.

"I had a yearbook and then burned it as an offering to the ancient ones."

"Sounds like high school was rough for you." He shut the yearbook.

"Patty and her ilk didn't make it any easier." I met his eyes. "I suppose you were the bee's knees in high school?"

Luke grinned at me. He had a small dimple in his cheek when he smiled. "I like the way you talk," he said. "It's a little old-fashioned. I wish I'd known you in high school. I'd have made you my girlfriend."

"You aren't going to make me do anything." I jerked back.

"Convince you, then."

"You're not my type."

"Hot?" His bottom lip caught in his teeth.

"Dumb. Pretty. Like a gas station muffin. We would not have hung out in high school."

"We might have. I was kind of a strange kid. I made the grave social mistake of moving to a small town and enrolling in high school in the middle of the semester. Never recovered." Luke slid the oversize book back on the shelf.

Downstairs, a door slammed.

Before I could inadvertently gasp, Luke grabbed me, pressing me against him and tucking us beside the bookcase.

The only sound was the thud of his heart, careful and slow.

Mine raced.

Should we make a break for it? It was a smoking gun if either Ricky or Heather caught me in Patty's bedroom.

We waited a minute then another.

Luke hissed out a low breath as Salem pranced to the master door and downstairs.

A man yelled, then there were heavy footsteps, and the door slammed.

"Your dog is a terrible guardsman," I whispered to Luke.

Pressing his huge body against the fancy wallpaper, he peered out the front window. "It wasn't the front door."

I peeked around his shoulder

He grabbed me. "Stay out of sight."

Ignoring him, I slowly pulled back the curtains.

In the front yard, Smokey was sniffing the air, tail slowly wagging.

"Someone was here," Luke whispered.

"No shit, Sherlock."

I tiptoed to the bathroom to peer out the back window.

"See anything?" he asked when I padded back out.

"No," I lied.

I had seen someone—a man who looked an awful lot like the fire chief.

CHAPTER 10

Luke

"We need to go," Lilith said.

"I still haven't finished looking for clues," I reminded her.

In the backyard, my gaze swept over the empty, pristine yard artfully blanketed by freshly fallen snow.

There were footprints—a man's footprints.

"You sure you didn't see anyone?"

She fixed me with her dark gaze. "Must have missed him."

"Hmm."

Grasping the railing on the back deck, I vaulted to grab hold of the edge of the roof of the garage then shimmied over to the window, using my boot to open it and swing my legs inside.

"Find anything?" Lilith's voice was melodic on the wind.

"Gasoline, lighter fluid, accelerant," I relayed then squeezed back out through the window and sprang to the porch.

"Parkour in my spare time," I told her.

"If you're trying to impress me, it's not working."

"You're a little bit impressed. Admit it."

She ignored the comment. "You found the murder weapon?"

"We can't say for certain. I'm sure a number of those people Patty had on her hit list have accelerant in their garages," I told her as we made our way back through the house.

"Back to square one," she said, locking the front door as quickly as she'd opened it.

Smokey bounded around me.

"You were supposed to be guarding," I told the dog. "Hey, Lilith, do you want to grab coffee?"

But Lilith had disappeared back toward the Christmas market without so much as a goodbye or a see you later.

"You need to stop throwing yourself at unattainable women," I told myself as I walked quickly back to the fire station.

I also needed to stop trusting Officer Browning and his band of incompetent misfits on this investigation.

"It's not an electrical fire," an exasperated Cliff was saying to the gaggle of police officers gathered in the fire station when I returned.

The cops whispered to each other.

"But that's our professional conclusion," Bobby declared.

"Well, it's wrong," I interjected, "because I tested it and found accelerant."

There was more muttering among the cops.

"What did the autopsy say?" I prompted.

More shuffling.

"Has the autopsy been started?" Cliff asked dryly.

"Look," I said, taking out my phone to show them a screenshot from the security footage. "We found someone messing with the cameras, probably a suspect. You might want to check it out."

After answering a medical call from a café where there were drunken seniors all over the floor, saving a man dressed as Santa who had driven his riding lawnmower into a ditch—yeah, he was drunk—and rescuing someone's pet cat that turned out to be a very angry possum wearing a vest, I clocked out and whistled to Smokey.

I should have gone home to sleep, since my next shift was the night shift. However, the murder nagged at me.

Was Ricky the culprit, as Lilith believed, or did someone else dislike Patty enough to kill her?

I pulled up Patty's hate list, reading the first name.

David Reed.

That was the alien guy. If I had to put money on a small-town murderer, the conspiracy theorist who believed in extraterrestrials was at the top of my list.

Smokey and I made our way through the Christmas market. As I breathed in the smells of the crisp winter air and pine, my shoulders relaxed.

I loved Christmas. Not because of nostalgia about childhood Christmases. Probably because I'd never had a wholesome Christmas. It was something magical, foreign, and unobtainable. I'd spent hours when I was a kid, day-dreaming about the perfect Christmases real families had.

Now I spent hours dreaming about how I was going to one day have my perfect Christmas with the dog and the wife and the kids.

Maybe with Lilith.

What if Lilith was the murderer and I just didn't want to admit it because I liked her?

The narrow alley behind Lilith's stall was darker and more cramped than I remembered. Lilith's wasn't the only storage unit on the alley.

Maybe Patty had had an altercation with David. He'd killed her and dragged her to Lilith's shed then set it on fire.

Most of the storage sheds were dark. Unhooking the flashlight from my utility belt, I shined the beam into the nearest shed window.

Shit, was that a person?

Screams erupted from the public path between the stalls. Flames shot up into the sky.

Sprinting around Lilith's stall, I skidded to a stop as a blast of flames singed my nose and chin. Cursing, I threw myself to the ground.

Smokey jumped over me and lunged.

I sprang to my feet in time to see Smokey snarling, teeth firmly grasping the sleeve of David Reed.

"Get it off! Get it off!"

The teenage girls, who moments ago had been screaming, were laughing and pointing their phones at him.

"Don't record me. I said don't record me!" David raged as he fumbled behind himself and grabbed a purple rod from his sales counter.

I grabbed his arm before he could hurl the weapon at the girls.

"Drop it," I growled as Lilith ran over.

"Lilith, help! Your boyfriend and his dog are trying to kill me," David yelped.

"He's not my boyfriend."

I shoved David to the ground.

"Here's your murderer, Lilith," I said to her as she grabbed Smokey's collar, dragging him back from David.

"I'm not a murderer," David protested.

"Yes, you are," I snarled. "I just saw another body in your storage shed. David's the murderer. He used that flame-thrower to kill Patty and hid the evidence in his storage shed. Call the police."

"Not yet," Lilith said. "Officer Girthman is incompetent and won't be able to force a confession."

"I didn't do anything!" David screeched.

Lilith gazed down at him thoughtfully. "I have a four-teenth-century French torture kit that I've been dying to use."

"Don't let her torture me, please!" David grabbed my arm.

"I won't if you tell us what the hell is going on."

"First, I want to see this body," Lilith said.

Yanking David by the collar of his jacket, I frog-marched him to his storage shed in the narrow alley.

Lilith's fingers briefly grazed my hip bone as she unhooked the flashlight from my belt then shined it into the shed window.

"I swear I don't know how a body got in my shed," David babbled while Lilith peered into the disorganized hut.

"We really should call the police," I began.

"And have you be the laughingstock of the force? I don't think the fire chief would forgive you." She smirked. "That is not a body."

"I told you!" David shouted.

"Then what is it?"

David turned red. "I like to cosplay. All the superheroes have padded suits."

"Keys." Lilith held out her hand.

David slapped his key ring into her palm.

The shed door opened with a creak. On the floor was a flesh-colored suit with padded foam muscles. Someone had airbrushed painted contours on the muscles to make them more lifelike and added tattoos.

"The tattoo," Lilith muttered, flipping over the suit.

"It's hard to gain muscle definition," David whined. "We're not all like your boyfriend. I have a job, you know. I can't spend all day working out and eating baked chicken."

"He's not my boyfriend."

I draped an arm around her shoulder. "She says after she was finding an excuse to cop a feel."

She turned her head to me. "Captain, we are in the middle of a murder investigation."

"I didn't murder anyone," David promised.

"But," Lilith, said her face darkening, "you did spray-paint the security cameras the night before the murder."

"You don't know that," David sputtered. "You can't know that. I was wearing a disguise!"

CHAPTER 11

Lilith

"**M**ystery solved. Now you can call the police, Captain."

"I didn't... You can't." David burst into tears and collapsed in the snow. "I can't go to jail."

I was unmoved. Patty was a horrible person, but she didn't deserve to die.

"Please don't call the police," David blubbered when Luke pulled out his phone. "I didn't block out the cameras to kill Patty. I was trying to keep her from spying on me. She was going to shut down my stall. Yours, too, Lilith. She was using the cameras to spy on people. She was threatening me about my"—he licked his lips—"late-night sales activity. So I know she was using the cameras to spy."

"Sounds like a pretty solid motive," Luke remarked.

"Honest, I wasn't going to kill her. Blood makes me queasy. I would never. Lilith, you remember? When you brought that roadkill to show-and-tell?"

"You did puke all over the walls," I concurred.

"I have notes she wrote me," David said, shoving his hand into his pocket and coming out with a crumpled piece of paper—the same custom notepaper from Patty's home office.

Luke took it and read, "'I know about the eggs you're selling.' What eggs?"

David's eyes flicked around. "Alien eggs."

"Uh-huh."

"They crash-landed here in Harrogate, and they left droppings."

"So you found them and are selling them at the Christmas market?" I raised an eyebrow.

David squirmed. "I'm selling replicas. I have to make an honest living. Besides, I would never actually hurt Patty. She's Heather's best friend. Heather would never forgive me."

"Heather can't stand you," I said slowly.

"Heather's never had a boyfriend. Not a real one anyway." David scoffed. "She's getting to that age where it's do or die. She's going to come crawling to me when she realizes that she just wants a nice guy with a good-paying job."

"You... run an alien stall." Luke was visibly confused.

"He works at Svensson PharmaTech and takes banked PTO during Christmas," I explained.

"Guys like me, we don't get picked the first go-around, but once a woman like Heather realizes that she's not getting a man like Ricky, she'll come begging me to go out with her," David said confidently. "If Ricky dumped Patty, then Heather would have been Queen Bee because she would have had a man and Patty wouldn't. Heather was going to be desperate for me."

Luke's mouth was a thin line. "You're disgusting."

"But not a murderer," David replied.

"Their marriage was on the rocks?" I asked.

"Oh yeah." David nodded.

"I thought they were going to try for a baby," I mused. Had Patty wanted to break it off but Ricky didn't, so he killed her?

"Can I leave?" David asked.

"Get out of here," Luke growled.

David scrambled up and scurried off.

Luke draped an arm around my shoulders and walked me back to my stall.

"You can go too," I told him, not sure if I was uncomfortable or welcomed the weight of his arm.

"I'm free now," he said, his hand moving to my lower back as we headed back into the stall.

Luke settled on a stool as I put water on to boil. "Back to square one."

"We can't even be sure that David wasn't the murderer," I said, setting two cups down on the silver tray. "Two days ago, he was screaming at Patty and threatening her."

"I think he's too much of a coward for that, like his convoluted game with Heather," Luke argued.

I poured the steaming water into the cups.

"Me? I prefer honesty," Luke said. "Just tell a woman what you want, how you feel."

I handed him a cup, and our fingers touched. I jerked my hand away.

Luke set down his cup and reached for my hand. "I like you, Lilith. I'd like to take you out on a date."

I froze, unsure what to say.

His lightly calloused fingers tipped up my chin. "See how easy it is to just say what you want?"

"And you want me."

"Yeah, Lilith, I do." There was sincerity in those blue eyes.

I turned away. "I told you you're not my type."

"Just keep an open mind," he replied, picking up the teacup, completely unperturbed by my rejection.

"I'm busy."

"We don't have to go right now. We could go out tomorrow."

"Go out where?"

"A surprise." His soft mouth formed a smile. "You can even bring Salem. Take a break from sleuthing. Come enjoy Christmas."

"I do not like Christmas." I picked up my cup.

"That's just because no one's really showed you the true meaning of the holidays. Salem likes Christmas," he said, bending down to pet the black cat, who had a stuffed catnip mouse in a green-and-red vest in his mouth.

I busied myself with realigning the crystal-and-herb-decorated candles on the shelves while Smokey panted noisily next to me and shoved his big, wet nose against my hand.

The dog barked when a drunken man stumbled into the stall.

"Been looking everywhere for you," Ricky slurred. "Just tell me."

Was the guilt finally taking hold?

"Tell you what?" I prompted.

"Tell me how you killed her."

"I didn't."

Ricky stumbled forward, grasping for me. "I know you did it. Not mad, just need to know."

Luke rose, his soft mouth now a hard line.

Somehow, he seemed bigger, broader, in the narrow stall.

"*Do not touch her.*" Luke shoved his large body between me and Ricky.

"I can take care of myself." I tried to move him aside, but I might as well have attempted to move a marble statue.

"Like you took care of Patty?" Ricky slurred.

"Get the fuck out of here," Luke growled at him.

"I know what you did." Ricky pointed at me. "I know it was you. Everyone in town knows it was you."

He stumbled outside into a snowdrift then pulled himself upright.

Luke stood at attention at the entry to my stall and watched Ricky drag himself into the crowded, active Christmas market.

"I'm going to stay here with you just in case he comes back," Luke said darkly.

My phone beeped.

"You'll be here by yourself."

"Hot date?" he snarled softly.

"Delivery. Some of us work for a living."

CHAPTER 12
Luke

My phone rang as I was arguing with Lilith about walking her to the house where she was making a delivery.

"Captain Reynolds," I barked into the receiver.

"Police are here," Cliff said, voice carefully measured. "They have the autopsy results."

"I'll be right there." I ended the call. "Lilith. Give me your number."

"No."

Grabbing a piece of paper, I scrawled my cell number on it and slapped it into her hand. "Fine. Be difficult. Call me when you make your drop-off and when you're back here."

Lilith fixed me with that dark-eyed gaze then wordlessly took the paper and stuck it in her pocket.

I would have walked with her, but she headed in the opposite direction from the fire station, and I really needed to know the results of the autopsy.

The papers were spread out over one of the long folding tables when I jogged up. Cliff stood at the head of the table, arms crossed. The chief paced around, running his hand under his chin.

"What do the results say?" I asked.

"Definitely murder," Eddie murmured.

I slowly read through the report. There were no signs of smoke inhalation, but there were several stab wounds on the body that had been discovered.

"What caused them?" I asked.

"Due to the amount of fire damage, it isn't conclusive yet as to cause of death. They have to send it out to the big city for a full investigation."

"The only thing you need to know," Officer Browning said to me, "is that Patty didn't die in the fire. So we don't need the fire department involved anymore."

"Someone set the fire to burn the body and cover up the murder," I argued. "The fire department still needs to be investigating this."

"No, you don't," Bobby snapped at me. "This is fully a police department matter."

"Chief?" I complained.

He sighed, rubbed his balding head, and put his ball cap back on. "You heard the man, Luke. I don't need a jurisdictional fight between you boys."

Bobby's chest puffed out, and the officers high-fived as they gathered up the papers.

Cliff made a disgusted noise.

Not bothering to grab my jacket, I strode after my uncle as he left the station.

"Are you serious?" I demanded, my boots crunching on the icy ground as I caught up to him. "You can't just let them have our case. It's a fire. We investigate fires. The police are just going to screw it up. Smokey knows more about fire investigation than Bobby."

The chief let out a loud sigh. "You're a captain now, Luke," he chided me, "and a lot of the job is political. I told you that when you got a promotion."

"A woman is dead, and there's a murderer loose," I said flatly.

"And the police will—"

"Bullshit," I spat. "Why are you doing this? Why aren't you fighting for this?"

"Sometimes this is how these things go."

"Something's up, isn't it? Is it the mayor? The city council? The Svenssons?"

"I told you, boy…" His whole body sagged. Suddenly my uncle seemed tired and old.

Not wanting to be the cause of him having some sort of health episode, I decided not to push it.

"Why don't you go try to get some rest? I know you have the night shift." Uncle Don clapped a hand on my shoulder.

Jaw clenched, I said, "I need to prep for my presentation to the first graders."

And I needed to figure out why someone would want to stab Patty to death, because I didn't trust the police to solve the murder.

CHAPTER 13

People gave me odd looks as I took a shortcut through the Christmas market, ducking around the vendors selling roasted-pecan clusters and paper cups of hot chocolate.

Scoffing, I thought about Luke and his request for a date.

He wanted to show me the spirit of Christmas? Was that some sort of euphemism for... well, you know?

I could admit that he was attractive in an all-American way. He would probably play the Nutcracker Prince if, for some reason, my life turned into a fever dream of a ballet recital.

Resting the heavy box on my hip, I checked my phone. No replies from Penny or Morticia, just like the last text messages I'd sent.

No doubt they were too busy with their boyfriends to respond to the, frankly, *inspired* photo I'd sent of a taxidermy mouse sharing tea with one of the now-illegal spider cookies at a miniature table.

Maybe I would see my sister and my friend more if I had a boyfriend. He'd be like an accessory—prop him up in a booth on a double date.

Why was I so concerned with dating? I was a grown woman. If this were the 1600s, I'd be considered to be almost at death's door. Far too old to find a man and have children.

I almost dropped the box. Salem meowed reproachfully from his spot on top of it, from which he surveyed the Christmas market.

Why in the world would I want a child—a snotty, crying, whining child?

Or an interesting, spooky child with dark hair and blue eyes?

Absolutely not.

I walked quickly on, ignoring a man in a Santa suit who waved a wreath at me.

Heather's Victorian house wasn't on as prominent a street or as big or as well-decorated as her friend Patty's was. I rang the doorbell, heard someone yell unintelligibly from inside, and waited a moment before I turned the brass knob and let myself in. Following the voices, I made my way to the large white kitchen at the back of the house.

"Good evening, Heather, Ashley, Anna."

"Hi, Lilith." Anna's tone was hot and angry. "I was just leaving." The café owner grabbed her bag. The strap caught on one of the stools and sent it crashing to the floor, but Anna didn't stop to pick it up. A few moments later, the front door slammed behind her.

"An early happy solstice to you all," I said.

"Ugh, why is Lilith here?" Ashley complained to Heather. Now that Patty wasn't around, Ashley was really letting her inner mean-girl dictator shine.

"I needed her spice mix for the Christmas punch. Anna wouldn't bring any," Heather explained. "You can just put it on the counter." Heather gestured with her rolling pin. Her lips were pursed as she flattened the dough.

"Can I help with anything for the funeral tomorrow?" I asked, righting the stool.

"Haven't you done enough?" Ashley snapped at me.

"I didn't kill your friend. If anything," I said, leveling my gaze at her, "you're more of a suspect than I am. Rumor has it that you're putting your hat in the ring to be the new chair of the Christmas committee."

"You are?" Heather cried. "But I'm the chairwoman pro tem."

"Yes," Ashley said, "but you're so busy with the funeral, taking care of Ricky, and making sure Patty has a holiday in her honor."

"I was a Girl Scout all the way through high school. I can multitask," Heather argued.

"You're grieving. You shouldn't have to take on all the chairwoman duties too." Ashley dabbed her eyes. "Poor Patty. I can't believe she's gone."

"Please," Heather snapped. "The day before she died, you were complaining that she didn't like the custom scrunchies you made for everyone."

"That was then. I'm above such pettiness now. We're supposed to be celebrating Patty's memory. The mayor confirmed we could put a shrine in the clock tower."

"Whatever. Just go make sure Tranquil Tulips hasn't lost the order," Heather said.

We stood there in silence after Ashley left.

"You seem to be the only person who's sad that Patty's gone," I told Heather.

"Her parents are upset," Heather said. "Well, her mom claims she is. Her dad is hamming it up, but as soon as Patty turned eighteen, he split from her mom to start a new family, so I don't know how sad he is when he's reminded of his old life. His wife is pregnant with twins. She's only six months older than Patty. I think he met her online." She shook her head. "Men. They're disgusting."

"Yes, such pigs."

Heather brought the rolling pin down with a crack on the chilled cookie dough then furiously rolled it out.

"Speaking of Ricky—" I began.

Whack came the rolling pin.

"How is he taking Patty's death?"

"He's in a period of delayed grieving," Heather said shrilly.

"I heard they were having marital troubles. I'm sure that must be complicated."

"She was so mean to him."

"I can imagine. But I thought she was in love with Ricky," I said.

"Patty never fully appreciated him for the man he was," Heather said reverently.

"I'm glad you'll be there to support him at the funeral. I'll be bringing stuffed mushrooms for the wake tomorrow," I promised.

"The more food, the better. It's going to be a full house, I'm sure. Vultures."

"The directions to make the Christmas-spiced punch are in the box," I told her, gathering up my cat and my bag.

"Thanks. Oh, Lilith?" Heather added. "I believe you."

"What?"

"I believe you didn't kill Patty."

"Then who did?"

"I don't know," she said determinedly, "but when they find out, I want you to burn them up in some sort of sacrificial offering."

CHAPTER 14

Luke

The high school marching band played a dirge as several uniformed firefighters and police officers slowly walked Patty's casket to the deep grave. The snow in the ancient cemetery had been cleared enough for the mass of townspeople to stream by to pay their respects.

While there were tears and sobbing, as was to be expected at a funeral, there were also a not-insignificant number of people, mostly my age, who didn't seem all that concerned that Patty was deceased.

There was no question in my mind that the murderer was here at the funeral. But who was it? There were the Svenssons, who had come to pay their respects. The mayor had given a speech at the church service about what a wonderful asset to the community Patty had been. That had earned a number of eye rolls and sarcastic comments, mainly from people from our high school class.

The uniformed officers lowered the casket into the ground. Family and friends filed past, tossing flowers onto the coffin.

I hung back.

The townspeople were all whispering behind their hands and glancing at me. It might have bothered a more sensitive person.

"... *heard she killed her...*"

"*Burned her alive...*"

Vultures. Heather was right. And they called me the weird one.

Luke was in the thick of the crowd, giving his condolences to Patty's family and friends and shaking hands with the town's more prominent members. When he approached Ashley, she threw herself into his arms like a Regency heroine.

Barf.

The cemetery was an old Victorian style with large trees and winding pathways. I always found cemeteries calming and peaceful. I liked to picnic in this one on warm nights.

"Hey, Lilith! Wait up."

Gravel crunched on the path as Luke approached me.

Pausing, I slowly looked him up and down. Crisp navy-blue fabric adorned with polished brass buttons, which he wore with a white shirt and black tie, draped his frame. The gold insignia of the Harrogate Fire Department gleamed in the winter sun. A sharp cap sat on his head. He grinned.

My gaze rested on his face. "Nice hat."

He touched it with a white-gloved hand then reached out to tug on a lock of my hair.

"For some reason, I almost expected you to wear rainbow colors to a funeral," he teased.

"Don't be silly. That would draw too much attention when trying to snoop."

Heather's house was packed. People spilled out into the yard. The receiving line to pay respects to the grieving widower and parents stretched into the street.

I hadn't been able to snoop when I'd dropped off the ingredients for the spiced punch. I wasn't going to wait in line for an hour just to get close to the house.

"Hey, you can't skip!" someone complained.

"Have to refresh the punch," I said, not stopping, holding up the paper sack of the spice blend I'd brought for that express purpose.

Inside the Victorian home, people were filling plates with funeral snacks and whispering speculations about Patty's murder.

I checked the spiced punch and added more rum and another handful of herbs, rubbing them between my palms to release the oil.

"Ricky, have you eaten anything today?"

Out of the corner of my eye, I saw Anna lead Ricky to the refreshment table. Ducking behind an oversize bouquet of flowers, I watched as Anna plated a selection of food for Ricky.

"These stuffed mushrooms are divine." She held one out between her fingertips and fed it to him.

His eyes never left hers as she slipped it into his mouth. Ricky grabbed her hand, his tongue darting out to lick her fingers before releasing them.

Anna's face was flushed. "Take care of yourself, okay?" She stretched up on her toes to embrace Ricky.

He wrapped his arms around her, pressing his face into her hair, then released her and returned to the receiving line in the next room.

Supportive neighbor, or was there something more between them?

The stuffed mushrooms, which I'd brought over early that morning needed to be refreshed. I headed into the kitchen, pulled out another tray of them from the fridge, and stuck them in the oven. I was keeping busy to make it look like I belonged while I catalogued the space.

When I carried the heated mushrooms back out into the living room, Ashley was practically ripping off her top in front of Luke. I experienced absolutely no jealousy while I scooped the steaming mushrooms onto a platter. I was above all of that.

"You better watch out."

I whirled around, the metal spatula raised.

Heather's expression was dark, her mouth twisted into a scowl as she jerked her chin toward Luke. "There are some girls whose sole purpose in life is to steal other people's men."

"You have a boyfriend?" Penny appeared at my side.

"Penny," I hissed.

"Sorry!" She bounced next to me then turned to Heather. "My condolences on your loss."

"Yes, it was a tragedy."

"Now that Patty's gone, Ashley's really come out of her shell, though," Penny added. "Garrett and I brought some gift cards for the family." She held up flowers and a dark-blue gift sack.

"You can leave those here," Heather said, escorting Penny to the gift table, which was laden with flowers and cards.

Ashley was still pawing at Luke. His blue eyes met mine.

I off-loaded the rest of the mushrooms then returned to the kitchen.

"I'm going to get more sparkling water," I said to no one. Dumping the tray in the sink, I kept walking through the kitchen, past the fridge.

Like many Victorian homes, this one had a small servants' staircase from the kitchen to the upper bedrooms. Taking them as quickly and lightly as possible, I hoped the hum of the visitors would mask any creaking of the ancient wood.

Not sure what I was looking for, I crept down the hallway. Patty and Heather had been best friends, right? That meant that Patty must have shared her blackmail scheme with her. Patty couldn't resist an audience.

The first two rooms were guest bedrooms. Heather wasn't married, nor did she have a boyfriend, to my knowledge. How was she able to afford such a large house? Probably rich parents. Wasn't that always how it happened?

The next bedroom was the master suite, decorated like an upscale version of a tween girl's pink bedroom. I prowled through it, opening drawers and snooping through the jewelry box. There was only one of the ubiquitous Christmas scrunchies. Also, the buckle didn't match anything in the closet. There wasn't anything related to the murder or the blackmail.

The next room was locked. Not for long.

"Christmas has come early," I murmured as I gazed around what could only be described as the Christmas committee's war room. One wall held an oversize map of the Christmas market, with potential violations flagged. My stall hosted a number of red pins. A whiteboard held the beginning plans for Patty's mayoral campaign. Circled in red text were the words *secret weapon* with a check mark beside them.

"Look who's caught red-handed. I should call the police." Luke walked into the room, letting out a low whistle. "This is what he meant," he murmured when he saw the whiteboard.

"Who?"

"Nothing."

"Tell me."

Luke looked away then back at me. "The chief warned me that I shouldn't get too invested in this case and that there are powerful political forces at work." He nodded to the whiteboard. "Hunter Svensson is married to the current mayor. He wouldn't like it if someone were to challenge her." Luke peered at me. "Aren't you friends with the Svenssons?"

"No. My friend is dating Garrett Svensson."

"They'd probably keep her in the dark about a murder."

"Surely they wouldn't murder someone just for running for mayor," I argued. "Wouldn't they just use their donations and clout in the community to crush her?"

"It's not just business with them. It's personal. She'd be going against Hunter's wife," Luke said. "You don't know how a man gets when someone is threatening the woman he loves."

Outside in the hallway, footsteps sounded.

Before I could formulate an excuse, Luke grabbed me, threw us out of the room, and closed the door. He pressed me against it, his huge body crushing me. One of his large hands cupped the back of my head. His forehead rested against mine while I drowned in his blue eyes.

"There you are." The footsteps stopped in front of us.

"Apologies, Heather," Luke said, pulling away while I tried to catch my breath.

The angry expression on Heather's face relaxed. "I thought I heard someone up here."

"Guilty as charged, ma'am." Luke flashed her that megawatt smile then took my hand.

Heather seemed to be expecting me to say something.

"Just taking your advice and trying not to let my man get stolen."

Heather stared intently. "I thought you said you weren't—"

"I actually did need to ask you something," I interrupted. "Do you know if Anna and Ricky are having an affair?"

"They're what?" She sucked in a breath.

"I saw them."

"*Saw them what?*" Heather's tone was possessive, jealous.

"Just hugging a little too long."

"I can't believe that. He wouldn't. Don't you ever speak about Ricky like that again. Ever."

CHAPTER 15

Luke

"You're not ready."

"Ready for what?" Lilith asked, not looking up from measuring out herbs onto an antique weighted scale.

"For our date."

Her spoon clattered to the counter. "I'm not going on a date with you."

"I think you are." I couldn't stop thinking about the way her smaller body had felt pressed against mine yesterday, the way her breath had quickened, the melting pools of her dark eyes. She wanted me.

"I'm busy."

"I have the perfect date planned." I leaned against the counter.

"There is no such thing."

Stepping behind the sales counter, I rested my hands on her hips.

There wasn't anything more I wanted to do than tip her head back and kiss her, but I wasn't sure whether she would kiss me back or claw my eyes out.

"You're going to be begging me to take you out."

"Doubtful."

I lifted my hand to run my fingers along the creamy skin of her neck, her pulse jumping under my thumb.

"We're going to convince the health department to let you sell your cookies."

"We are?"

"The health inspector is a Christmas-loving woman, and she likes me. She thinks I'm cute." I smirked.

Lilith scowled.

I ran my thumb over her mouth. "I expected you to be happy that I'm helping to rescue you from your Christmas cage and let you run free among the holiday baked goods."

"What's the catch?"

"This is a date, Lilith. I like you; I want to spend time with you. There is no catch." Except for the fact that I wanted to kiss her then take her in the back of my truck.

"Fine." She grabbed her oversize black leather bag. "Let's go on the date."

"Not so fast."

She scowled again at my lazy grin.

"You're not dressed for a date." I unzipped my back-pack and pulled out a bright-red Mrs. Claus outfit that I'd found in the Christmas market. It had a red-velvet fur-lined cropped jacket to go over a short red dress with a flared skirt.

"I assume you already have black boots." I handed it to her.

Lilith hissed and recoiled like a cat. "No date."

"I told you." I hung the outfit up on the door of the little changing room in her stall. "Inspector Ada is a fellow Christmas lover. You have to let your holiday cheer shine. Or… you could watch as other people clean up this Christmas, Santa dumping loads of money in their stalls while they sell overpriced Christmas cookies to tourists."

"I thought firefighters were supposed to be good guys." Lilith snatched the outfit off its hook and retreated to the small changing room.

Even though it didn't have standard Christmas-market decor, Lilith's stall was still warm and cozy. Tall beeswax candles, their flames flickering, put off a subtle and perfumed warmth. Dark velvet drapes adorned with shimmering silver stars lined the witchy-themed stall. There were antique wooden shelves adorned with crystal balls that seemed to hold secrets, ornate cauldrons emitting an eerie, colorful mist, and jars filled with dried herbs and curious ingredients. She'd made a few nods to the yuletide season with the Santa hats on the skulls, some red-and-gold candles, and sprigs of mistletoe.

Salem dropped a mouthful of dried herb leaves next to my hand.

"Is that a present for me?" I stuck one of the leaves into the flame and watched intently as it was engulfed. The sweet smell of smoke wafted in the air, and Lilith appeared out of the small changing room.

"You look—"

"Stupid."

"Hot."

"Your Christmas fetish is disturbing," she said, closing the bifold door of the changing room. Lilith fluffed out the skirt. "It's not even that short. I can't imagine what you find arousing."

Everything.

After pulling out a box, Lilith started loading it with cookies.

"Not the spider cookies," I told her.

"That's what I'm selling," she protested.

"We're trying to brand you as just a humble small-town, Christmas-loving girl who was wronged by an overzealous Christmas committee," I replied as I tied a big red ribbon in her dark hair. "You need to bake festive, wholesome cookies. I'll help you. Let's go to your commercial kitchen."

'"No need." She bent down behind her sales counter.

I leaned over to see what she was messing with.

"You're baking your cookies here?" I asked as she rearranged the racks on a mini oven. "Maybe let's not tell the health department that information."

"Of course I don't bake them all here," she replied, opening up the mini fridge. "I could never get the volume. I use the shared kitchen space at the Rural Trust incubator. But people like watching me bake and decorate while they shop." She slammed the mini fridge door closed. "It's part of the holiday experience."

After sprinkling flour onto an oversize wood cutting board, she used a heavy rolling pin to roll out the dough into a thin sheet.

I stuck another of the dried herb leaves into the fire and was mesmerized as it burst into flames.

"So you burn things for fun?" she asked.

"And take pretty girls out on dates."

She sniffed. "So that's why you became a firefighter—because you love fire?"

"I find it fascinating," I admitted. "It's almost magical. There's like this innate human desire to be near flames but not too close. It's like a toxic relationship. I don't really do much firefighting now. Not like when I was a forest firefighter."

"A hotshot."

I winked at her. "You said it."

"It's the technical term," she sputtered as she set out a metal cookie tray.

"I was always constantly on with forest firefighting. Fires can linger for days then erupt and engulf everything. Kind of like with you."

"I don't engulf things," she said as she used a small dowel to draw on the cookie dough.

"Maybe more my desire for you." I leaned against the counter.

"Should have known you'd be obnoxiously cheesy."

"I think I wanted you from the moment I saw you. I just didn't know it at the time."

"I highly doubt that." She looked up at me.

"I told you I don't have time for bullshit," I said, leaning forward. "I get enough of that in the fire department. It doesn't have to be that complicated. I like you. I think you're cool. I want to date you and definitely want to fuck you. Shoot, I might even marry you."

Lilith opened a drawer and pulled out a long, sharp knife.

I sucked in a breath and took two quick steps back, almost tripping over Smokey, who yelped.

Lilith smirked then, using the sharp knife, expertly cut the dough into shapes as perfectly as if she'd used a cookie cutter.

"How do you know how to do that?" I asked cautiously, creeping back over to the counter where she worked.

"I'm a metalwork artist when I'm not trying to make it in the Harrogate Christmas Market. Cookie dough is a lot easier to work with than plate steel."

I couldn't quite make out what the shapes were— one looked like a Christmas tree, maybe with presents underneath.

"Did your mom bake cookies?" I asked her as she rolled the dough scraps into a ball and made a few rectangles.

"No, my mother left to join a commune when my sister and I were little." She slid the tray into the oven.

"Jeez, I'm sorry."

"My grandmother raised me."

The stall was filled with the scent of freshly baked cookies.

"My parents were pretty checked out too," I said. "My dad was already married to someone else when my mom got pregnant, and she really wanted a baby. Not so much a gangly teen boy with a bad attitude."

"I can't imagine you were that bad," Lilith commented. "What? Did you put up the Christmas tree the second week of December and not the first?"

"Ha-ha. More like I got into fistfights with her boyfriends."

The timer dinged, and Lilith pulled out the tray of cookies.

"Those aren't typical sugar cookies," I said as she slid them onto a cooling rack.

"They're infused with herbs—rosemary, a little thyme, honey." She broke off a piece of a long, skinny cookie and handed it to me.

I closed my eyes. It tasted like Christmas, but there was a hint of something darker, smokier. "These are so good. You should sell them."

"That's the plan." She tossed a cookie scrap to Smokey, who barely chewed it before gulping it down.

Lilith had a steady hand as she drew a cat sleeping in front of a Christmas tree on one cookie. With the big red bow in her hair, the animals crowding around her begging for a treat, the warmth of the candles, the strands of Christmas lights, and the red-and-white Christmas outfit, she was a Victorian Christmas card come to life.

And she looked like everything I had ever wanted.

I smiled at her softly. "For someone who hates Christmas, you sure are good at it."

CHAPTER 16

"This is demeaning," I huffed, my breath a steam cloud in front of me.

Ever since I'd put on the Christmas outfit, I'd caught Luke watching me like I was a cookie he wanted to savor.

"Really? Because you look like my deepest, darkest Christmas fantasy come to life." Luke's bottom lip caught in his teeth.

I pretended to be annoyed. The part of me that I never allowed to be a gooey-eyed teen girl was thrilled by his attention.

"If my grand plan doesn't work, you can turn me into a skin suit for your wall. But," Luke added, his hand resting on my waist, "if it does work, then you have to let me take you out for a real first date."

The historic city hall building was an architectural marvel back in the day, when Harrogate had been a New England industry town. Its grand facade was bathed in the warm glow of countless twinkling lights. Garlands and wreaths adorned with red ribbons cascaded down its ornate columns.

Luke opened the oversize glass-and-steel doors for me. My boots echoed on the marble floor of the grand entry hall. The atrium had been transformed into a winter wonderland, with festive displays and a crackling fireplace. To one side was a towering Christmas tree bedecked in multicolored lights and oversize baubles.

"We'll go fast so you don't melt," Luke promised, escorting me up the grand staircase to the second floor, where the various city department heads had their offices.

It was clear which was the health inspector's because it was practically dripping with Christmas decor.

Inspector Ada cooed when she saw the handsome firefighter.

"Give me some sugar. Luke, come over here. How is my favorite hero?" The older woman pulled him down to noisily kiss his cheeks.

"Trying not to drive my truck through the police station."

"Not everyone can be as smart and handsome and brave as you." She fussed with his collar. "What can I do for you, Luke?"

"I was hoping you could help out my—"

"*Ooo!*" Ada squealed and clapped her hands. "Luke, did you finally find yourself a little girlfriend?" Ada clasped me to her ample bosom. "What a cute little thing you are. I wish I still had a waist like that. I hope you know how to cook," she said in mock seriousness, "because Luke knows how to eat."

"Of course I know how to cook," I said then added for more effect, "I'm making him steak, shrimp, and garlic-herb-and-bacon mashed potatoes for dinner tonight. And green beans."

Ada let out a belly laugh. "This is a girl who is not letting her man wander."

"I also brought cookies to celebrate the holiday season." I held out the box.

"How cute. I love Christmas cookies."

"Lilith makes amazing cookies," Luke said, a dopey expression on his handsome face.

"Okay, girl! I see how she reeled you in, Luke."

"Unfortunately," Luke said, smoothly transitioning into his ask, "the Christmas committee issued her a citation, and she's not allowed to sell those amazing cookies."

"A citation? The Christmas committee is really working overtime and has been making my job difficult this holiday season with all these complaints," Ada said. "And we're not even halfway through December!"

"It's Christmas, right?" Luke said passionately. "You can't have Christmas without Christmas cookies."

"You most certainly cannot, and what adorable cookies these are. Let me just pull up this citation, and I'll take care of this right now."

Ada typed on her keyboard then took a bite of one of the cookies. "Yummy! These are delicious. I've never had a cookie that tasted like that."

"So glad you enjoy them. I'll have to bring some more," I promised.

"Citation?" Ada asked.

I handed her the printed ticket.

"Stall 666. Hmm."

Luke rocked on his heels.

"Let's see here... citation issued for selling Christmas cookies individually wrapped but baked on-site—"

"They're baked at the Rural Trust shared kitchen and packaged there," I interrupted.

"And a cat on the premises," Ada continued.

"He keeps the rats away."

"Notes say Lilith was belligerent. Oh, you're *Lilith*," Ada said, turning to glare at me. "The murderer. You don't look like the spawn of Satan."

"Of course I didn't murder Patty," I said quickly. "We were old school chums. Go way back. She meant well—she was having a bad day. Marital problems. You know how it is."

"Don't I know it," the older woman said loudly. Ada gave Luke a look. "You always did have a soft spot for rejects."

"I'm converting her," he said seriously.

"Luke is a hero for keeping the rest of the Christmas market from burning down." Ada regarded me critically. "I can tell he really is getting you into the Christmas spirit. When I come down to your stall, I want to see Christmas cheer and a pristine selling environment. Then I won't have any problem voiding this citation."

"And no cats," I promised.

"Keep the kitty. I love cats. Have eight of them."

"That was always my plan," I told her.

"Now you have Luke, and you'll have eight kids!" Ada said happily.

It was a struggle in self-control not to make a face. "Yes. So many children."

"You have a fine young man there." Ada took my hand. "You don't want to end up like me—ex-husband number three and not a baby to show for it."

Luke was whistling "Have Yourself a Merry Little Christmas" along with the carol that filtered out of the sound system. Once we stepped onto Main Street, which had been closed to traffic for the Christmas market, Luke grabbed me around the waist and danced in time to the music.

"You're almost in the clear," he said, picking me up and spinning me around.

Several onlookers applauded.

"No, I'm not. Ada's going to come by the stall and see that it's not a Christmas vomitorium. She already thinks I cast a spell or something to reel you in."

"No spells needed," Luke said, resting a hand on my waist and tugging me toward him.

"Where am I going to get enough Christmas decorations to meet her standards?" I worried. "Maybe I should just borrow someone else's stall for an afternoon. No, she'd notice."

"Sounds like someone needs some hot chocolate."

"Only if there's alcohol in it," I said darkly.

Luke laughed. "This is Harrogate. Of course the hot chocolate is spiked."

He led me over to a nearby stall where the menu was written in fancy chalk script.

"Two gingerbread hot chocolates, please," Luke said to the lady behind the counter.

She slid two steaming novelty mugs over to him. Luke handed me one.

"The first step into your new life as a Christmas fanatic. Cheers."

I blew on the hot chocolate.

Luke didn't, though, and just took a big swallow of the scalding liquid.

"Hotshot," I teased.

His tongue darted out to lick his lips. He leaned in. The snow fell gently, settling on his shoulders and in his hair. Despite my skepticism about the holiday, I was feeling warm and fuzzy inside. With the twinkling Christmas lights and the smell of gingerbread, I could almost see why he loved the holidays so much. Or maybe it was just him.

Luke set the mug down on a nearby ledge then cupped my face. The air seemed to thicken with anticipation. The masculine scent of him, smoky and dark, mixed with the subtle fragrance of pine from the nearby Christmas tree.

Our lips met beneath the snowy sky. It was soft and tentative, like the delicate snowflakes that drifted around us.

"See?" he breathed after I broke the kiss. "I told you Christmas could be pretty awesome."

CHAPTER 17
Luke

"It won't take too much work to turn this place into a winter wonderland," I remarked when we were back in Lilith's stall.

"Your toxic positivity is grating. Spooky is my whole aesthetic. When is Inspector Ada even coming by? Where am I going to find enough decorations to make a tasteful Christmas stall? Between my storage shed burning down and being banned from selling cookies, I'm dead in the water," Lilith fretted.

"It just has to look Christmassy enough. Shoot, just bake a bunch of cookies, get a couple of trees up, and you're good to go." I wrapped my arms around her, tilted her head up, and kissed her just because I could.

Lilith melted in my arms. She was still in that red dress, and I wanted to unwrap her like a Christmas present.

"I'll be here when Ada comes by," I promised. "She's not going to fail my girlfriend when I'm there."

"Your girlfriend?" She seemed shocked.

"Why not?"

"Because…"

My phone rang.

"Let me take this while you try to think of a good excuse. Captain Reynolds."

"Dude, you need to get back to the station."

"What's up, Cliff?" I asked, moving to the stall's entry.

"You know how the police were going to get the big-city morgue to do an autopsy? Well, they found something."

"I'm guessing it's not a signed confession."

"Almost," Cliff said. "Patty was definitely stabbed, and they know the murder weapon. It was a long, sharp dagger or ice pick, but get this—it has some sort of decorative piece on it because they found melted glass and glitter."

Hmm. Long decorative knives… or maybe hatpins decorated with spooky spiders?

"I hear you. Thanks for letting me know. I'll head right over."

"A break in the case?" Lilith asked.

I tensed as she appeared beside me. She had taken off the cropped red jacket and replaced it with an oversize black-and-gray woven shawl.

I hesitated. I shouldn't tell her. In light of this new information, she was a suspect, wasn't she?

Three minutes ago, you wanted her to be your girlfriend.

"Uh, yes," I said, sticking the phone in my pocket. "They've determined the murder weapon. It was some sort of long, thin metal dagger that was decorated with glass ornamentation."

Both of us looked at the collection of spooky antique hatpins displayed on a wooden rack.

Lilith's dark eyes narrowed.

"You think I actually am the murderer." Her tone was sharp. "All of this—the dating, the kiss—was all to try to get close to me to get more information, wasn't it?"

"Are you kidding me?" I shook my head. "I did that because I like you. It doesn't have to be that dramatic."

CHAPTER 18

Lilith

"You're back!" Penny bounded into the stall. "Hi, Salem. Oh!" My friend clapped her hands to her mouth. "Whoopsie! I didn't know you were busy." She started to back out of the stall with a maniacal grin on her face.

"Luke was just leaving," I said.

At the same time, Luke said, "I have to go back to the fire station."

There was an awkward pause.

"I'll see you around, Lilith," Luke said finally and loped out of the stall.

"Your commentary is not needed," I said when he'd gone.

"Oh my god, Lilith." Penny grabbed my arm, jumping up and down. "Do you like him?"

"No. Can't stand him."

"And you're wearing a Christmas dress? You must *really* like this guy."

"It's part of my disguise to manipulate the city officials into letting me sell cookies again." I grabbed my shapeless black dress and went into the small changing room.

I took off the red dress and leaned against the wall. Why had I let Luke kiss me? Hadn't I already learned my lesson? Guys like him didn't like girls like me. I knew that. Luke wanted something. He had kissed me to try to get me off-balance, fishing for information.

Too bad I had told Inspector Ada that I was going to cook for him tonight. Fuck me and my big mouth. Why couldn't I have a nice, quiet Christmas? Why was there so much drama? Between the kiss and Patty and her mean-girls harassment, it was just like high school all over again.

"You will never kiss Luke Reynolds again," I whispered to my reflection in the antique silver mirror.

When I came back out of the changing room, feeling like my old self, Morticia was waiting with Penny.

As much as it hurt that Luke might think I was responsible for the murder, that was preferable to his thinking Morticia had done it.

"Sister," I greeted my twin.

"Sister." She kissed me on the cheek. Normally stoic and unflappable, my sister seemed nervous.

You do not think your own sister is a murderer.

But... she had been wearing a hat that day. I'd also seen her butcher a chicken, she'd taken an ice sculpture class that one time, and I'd seen her wield an ice pick.

"What was it?" I asked.

"Sister?"

"What were you going to tell me? You were going to tell me something right before Patty was discovered."

Morticia sighed and fidgeted with her lace cuffs.

"You killed Patty, didn't you?" I asked, reaching under the counter for a bag. "We're going to have to spirit you out of the country. Penny, go find that boyfriend of yours. Surely he can assist us in purchasing a villa in a nonextradition country where Morticia can live out the rest of her days in exile. I don't trust Jonathan to be able to manage that."

"Lilith—"

"I'm not mad, Sister. We can work this out. Unfortunately, time is of the essence. The authorities know. The police aren't that incompetent. They have an autopsy report detailing how Patty was murdered. Luke's already linked you and me to the hatpins. I'm sure—"

"No, Lilith. That wasn't what I came to tell you."

I paused.

Morticia grimaced. "I didn't kill Patty, Lilith. I'm pregnant."

Penny screamed. "You're going to be a mom!"

"Penny, get ahold of yourself," I snapped.

Morticia winced. "You're upset. You've been mad for years since I started dating Jonathan."

"I'm not mad." I put the bag back. "You found a useless idiot with money to manipulate. Good for you. You're a beacon of hope to us all in these dark times."

"You don't like that I've been spending so much time with him," my sister pressed.

"She has Luke now," Penny said. "The tables will turn, and we're hardly going to see her."

"The only tables turning are going to be my torture tables if Luke storms in here to try to have my sister and my future niece hauled off to jail," I swore. "I am not angry. This is wonderful news, Sister. I've always wanted to be the spinster aunt. And now we'll have a wonderfully clever little girl in the family."

"You know you're having a girl?" Penny gasped.

"I do not." Morticia frowned.

"She better."

"We don't know, Lilith."

"Where are my cards, Salem? The cards!" I snapped my fingers at the cat.

He meowed and nosed the tarot card deck toward me.

"Sit." I pulled out one of the small metal chairs for Morticia then lit several candles and some dried sage.

I shuffled the cards then had her cut the deck.

Penny leaned over my shoulder as I dealt them out.

"The Empress, resplendent in fertility and motherhood, graces the spread with her presence," I said as the candle sputtered. "Her nurturing energy radiates, intertwining with the High Priestess, who guards the secrets of intuition and the unseen. The Queen of Cups, an emblem of maternal love, emerges as the final affirmation. Yes, you will be having a daughter."

I wafted the sage smoke around Morticia.

"Now, Penny," I said as Morticia studied the cards, "put that expensive journalism degree to good use and find anything that can get Morticia an alibi."

"And a copy of the autopsy report so that we can get ahead of refuting any evidence they might have against Morticia," Penny added.

"No need. I know who can get that for us." I smiled.

"You can't just come here and demand the autopsy report."

Officer Girthman flinched as I raised my hand. Then I jabbed my nail on the tip of his nose. "I have photos from the school dance in eighth grade—"

"This is blackmail!" he sputtered.

I smiled.

He gulped.

"It's only blackmail if I tell you that if you don't give me a copy of the report, then those photos are going to be all over the Harrogate Facebook page. But of course I'd never do that."

"Okay, fine. But I have to scan it when no one is looking."

"Thirty-six hours," I warned him.

CHAPTER 19
Luke

I didn't want to believe Lilith was the murderer. But what about her twin sister? Would Morticia kill to protect her twin?

I didn't share any of my suspicions with the rest of the crew. The police told us that we weren't supposed to be on the investigation anymore. Therefore, they could race around like Christmas geese avoiding the oven.

I used the time to search for my missing good luck charm, deal with three slip and falls, two traffic accidents, one heart attack that turned out to be gas, and an untold number of drunks—drunks falling into snowdrifts, drunks stumbling into the wrong house and passing out, and drunks calling for a free ride so they didn't have to trudge home through the snow.

It was late when my shift finally ended. Lilith hadn't contacted me at all. Not that she'd have any reason to. It was probably over with her before it had even begun.

The Christmas market was dark as I took the shortcut through to my condo building. The only people out were the last of the service workers going home from closing down the bars and late-night restaurants.

Smokey was alert, ears up, pacing a few steps ahead of me. Suddenly, he paused, nose pointing straight ahead.

"Hey! Stop!" a woman yelled.

I couldn't tell exactly where in the market it was coming from.

Smokey knew.

I sprinted after the dog, who was growling as he raced through the dark, narrow pathways that wove between the shuttered stalls.

We turned a corner. At the end of the pathway were three people struggling. A figure in a long black trench coat and a ski mask took off running. I pursued him, but he jumped on an electric bike and raced off.

I jogged back to the two people who had been attacked.

"Lilith?" I reached for her. "Are you hurt? What happened? Who was that?"

"I'm fine." She shrugged me off and started to help Anna to her feet.

"Leave her on the ground," I ordered, jumping into EMT mode.

"I'm not one of those drunk senior citizens, Captain Reynolds," Anna said, pushing my hands away. "I just slipped on the ice in surprise. I'll be fine."

Salem appeared from the shadows and wound his way around my feet then rubbed his head against Anna's arm.

"Some help you were," Lilith told the cat.

"We should call the police." I pulled out my phone.

"No, no, I'm fine," Anna begged. "And you're never going to catch who it is. I don't need to be the topic of town gossip."

"Why are you two out so late at night?" I growled.

"Uh, just…" Anna stammered.

"I was actually coming to bring you dinner," Lilith said defiantly.

She stalked over to pick up a metal container, then she shoved it at me.

I opened the top partway. "It smells delicious." I leaned in and kissed her on the nose then kissed her mouth.

Her skin was warm against my cheek. If Anna hadn't been standing there, I'd have told Lilith I wanted her to come back to my place.

"I can't believe you made me dinner," I murmured against her neck.

"It's for my health department case. Take a picture and send it to Ada."

"You're a little holiday housewife." I kissed her again.

"Never."

"Admit it. You like me."

Anna coughed delicately.

Lilith jumped away from me. "I'm just going to take Anna home and make sure she's okay. Enjoy your dinner."

"I'm coming too," I insisted.

Even though I wanted to have my arm around her, Lilith walked ahead of me with Anna, the two women talking in the dark.

"I just don't understand what happened," Anna said as we headed to her apartment a few blocks over from Main Street.

"Did the attacker say anything to you?" I asked.

"No." She shook her head, looking back at me. "I was heading home, and out of nowhere, he lunged at me. It seemed like he was going to hit me. Then I heard Lilith yelling, and the guy ran off."

"Do you have any stalkers? An ex-boyfriend or anyone else who might want to hurt you?" I asked.

"Not that I can think of. Maybe it was just someone playing a prank."

I made a mental note to pull the security footage. It would probably have been better to call the police so that they would have a record. What if the attacker and the murderer were the same person? Also, it was suspicious that Anna didn't want to call the police.

I could have pressed the issue with Lilith, except that she'd made me dinner, and I really wanted to get laid.

"This is me," Anna said brightly, stopping in front of an old industrial building that the Svenssons had converted into lofts.

What if one of them had targeted Anna? Or what if it was a case of mistaken identity? There were too many unknowns.

Lilith stood next to me in the softly falling snow as we made sure Anna got into her building safely. Then I kissed Lilith for real. My tongue slipped into her mouth, and she let me tilt her head back so that I could kiss her deeply.

"I want you," I murmured against her mouth.

My hands slid up under the black coat she always wore. Her skin was warm under the wool, and if I slipped my finger into her tights, I was sure I'd find dripping-wet heat. Lilith moaned against my mouth as I cupped her tits through her sweater.

"Why are you kissing me?" she whispered when I released her. "Don't you think I'm a murderer?"

"Same reason I like fire. The danger is half the fun."

CHAPTER 20

Lilith

L uke leaned in to press his mouth against mine once more.

It had been a while since I'd been with a man. Scratch that. It had been five years since that Samhain concert with an emo boy who smelled like stale pumpkin. Luke was the exact opposite of that boy—muscular, tall, broad shoulders—and he wasn't a deathly pale lich of a human being.

Also, I had a feeling Luke would be way better in bed, but to be fair, any sex experience was going to be better than a quickie on a bedroll out in the middle of nowhere under the light of a full moon. Yeah, it sounded romantic and spiritual until you were pulling leaves out of your vagina and wondering if you had frostbite on your pinky toe.

"Since you brought me dinner, is that a subtle sign that you're going to let me eat you out?" Luke asked, his voice lowering an octave.

"Whoa, okay, I guess men these days are way more sex positive."

"I'm in my thirties. I don't have time for the 'Is she interested, or is she not' game. I want to fuck you. I want to feel your tight little cunt around my cock, and I want to make you come until you're singing Christmas carols."

My cheeks felt hot in the cold night air. "I doubt you're that good."

His smile was toothy and wolfish. "Give it a try before you say no."

"I have to wake up early to man the stall," I said, suddenly feeling shy.

It was the middle of winter. I was about as ungroomed as Salem when he woke up after a nap, and besides, did I really think it was a good idea to sleep with Luke? I mean, honestly, was I some sort of horny teenager?

"Maybe I should lay out some tarot cards and do an astrology reading first," I muttered.

"It's like that, then," Luke said, a smile playing around his lips. "What's the tarot card for? To see if I think you have great tits?"

"Is that how they let you talk in the force?"

"The person who has taxidermy mice arranged in festive party poses is worried about people's delicate sensibilities?" he asked as we started walking away from Anna's building. "Or she's stalling."

"I'm not stalling."

"You don't have to be scared of me," he said, his blue eyes almost as dark as the wintry night sky. "I have a feeling you bite more than I do."

* * *

After spending several hours removing my winter coat, so to speak, I lay in bed in the slightly chilly attic space that was my bedroom, wondering if I had blown my shot. What if someone else—someone like Ashley—showed up at the fire station tomorrow with even better food than what I had made then Luke decided that he'd rather be with her than me?

"You're being paranoid and crazy." I flopped over onto my stomach. It didn't help that I couldn't sleep. Every time I closed my eyes, I replayed Luke saying he wanted to fuck my tight little cunt.

"Okay, that's it." I threw off the covers.

Salem hopped down from his perch at the window.

"We're going into the woods."

* * *

The forest was silent and snowy as I parked the hearse at the trailhead and grabbed a chain saw out of the trunk.

Suspicious? Maybe, but I wasn't burying a body. Hearses had massive amounts of cargo space. Which was much needed, since I was in the woods to find some Christmas cheer—or at least some decorations.

Pulling the sled behind me, Salem riding on it, I entered the ancient forest and searched for low-hanging branches. Yes, you could buy garland in the Christmas market. But fresh was better.

And no, I was not stealing. This land belonged to Morticia's future brother-in-law, Matt Frost. And after Jonathan had impregnated my sister, I deserved some free greenery.

Maybe Penny was right, I thought as I sawed through a branch. Maybe I did need a boyfriend. Otherwise, Morticia and I would have less and less in common, and we'd only see each other on, well, Christmas, which was a family-obligation holiday. She was going to have a big, warm house with lots of children. Jonathan seemed like the type to want more.

Meanwhile, I would be the weird aunt with all the cats who would get annoying questions like *When are you going to get a boyfriend?* And *Why do you have so many cats?* It wasn't like I had a line of men waiting to court me or whatever the kids called it these days.

But there was Luke.

I threw the branch onto the sled and started on the next one.

Luke just wanted to sleep with me. He didn't actually *like* me, right?

Midmorning, I was nursing my third cup of black tea when I showed up at the stall. There wasn't a lot of traffic—usually, the tourists didn't start until the lunch rush. Someone had already started setting up my stall.

"Morticia?" I asked, stepping inside the dark building. The lights hadn't been turned on nor the candles lit. I stepped behind the sales counter.

"Lilith." Luke stood up slowly. His hand quickly hooked his flashlight onto the utility belt he wore.

"Looking for something?"

His smile was easy, disarming. "Yes, you."

He took me in his arms, walking me backward. My back bumped against the hard edge of the wooden counter.

I'd done a tea leaf reading at four that morning, and it said I was going to have unexpected visitors. On the off chance that it was Ada, I'd borrowed a red sweater dress from Penny. I didn't quite have her cleavage, but it was festive enough for my purposes.

"I really need to make the stall more festive—"

Luke silenced me with a kiss. The kiss was hard and hungry, like he'd stayed up all night, waiting to press his lips to mine. His tongue swept into my mouth, and I moaned softly. I was breathing hard as he broke the kiss to nuzzle my neck and pull at the sweater dress.

"Did you wear that just for me?" His deep voice was rough.

"I told you—for business."

"That's your go-to excuse, but I bet part of you is trying to get me really turned on because you secretly want me to bend you over that counter, spread your legs, and shove my thick cock into your tight little cunt."

He pulled down the collar of the sweater dress and my black bra. I stifled a loud moan as he sucked on my breast, teasing my nipple with his tongue until it was pebble hard.

"Let me show you how much I want you."

My legs spread inadvertently as he knelt down in front of me. Luke pulled out a knife from his utility belt then winked. Fabric ripped as he sliced through the black tights and my panties. Then his fingers were there, making me gasp.

"Too cold? Guess I'll have to use my mouth." His tongue was hot as it flicked against my slit.

This sure is escalating quickly, I thought but then didn't think anymore as his mouth pressed between my legs, licking me, sucking my clit. His tongue dipped into my opening. My fingers tangled in his thick blond hair as I bit back a moan.

Large hands dug into my thighs as he spread my legs wider, half holding me up for better access. It was quicker than I wanted—I could have stayed there with him giving me that kind of pleasure for, well, maybe not forever but for a while. Too soon, my legs were tightening, and I was tumbling over the edge.

I gasped, "Deep fry a newt, that was—"

"Lilith?" someone asked.

I kept my hand in Luke's hair, preventing him from standing up. I was already the hot topic of gossip in my small hometown. I did not need to add gasoline to the fire and have more rumors start that somehow I was using my witchy magic to seduce the fire captain and throw the case.

I cleared my throat, my face still hot from the orgasm. My legs trembled as I gripped the counter.

Heather moved closer, suspicion on her face. Just because she had been nice to me over the last few days—well, not nice per se but not mean—didn't mean that I could let my guard down. Once a mean girl, always a mean girl.

Using my knee, I pressed Luke's large body into the lower cabinets.

"Is someone here?" Heather asked.

"Of course not. I work alone."

Her nostrils flared.

"How can I help you? We're still trying to finish setting up."

"You and who?" Her expression was sour.

I pointed at Salem, who paused from licking his paw to meow at her. Heather relaxed slightly.

"So, how can I help you?" I repeated, hoping she would say *Never mind* or *Just checking in* and leave already.

She blinked rapidly then stammered, "A séance."

"A séance?"

"Yes, I'd like you to host a séance."

"For…"

"I want to speak with Patty."

"Not a problem. I will set up, and we can schedule that for tonight. Maybe she'll be able to give us a clue about her murderer."

"I'm bringing several people," Heather said rapidly. "I know that all that witchy stuff is nonsense, but I think Patty was murdered by someone she knew, and the séance might help make one of them confess."

"Are you going to bring the whole town?" I asked.

"Of course I'm not bringing the whole town, Lilith." Heather's voice was shrill. "Just have the séance ready. Eight p.m." She stormed out of the stall.

Unexpected visitors indeed. But had the tea leaves been referring to Heather or to Patty's ghost?

CHAPTER 21
Luke

"A séance? This town is batshit crazy."

"Séances make me good money," Lilith told me as she flitted around. She seemed nervous or apprehensive.

I grabbed her, my hands digging into her as I kissed her hard. It had taken a not-insignificant amount of self-control not to spread her legs and fuck her pussy right there on the counter, especially since she still had a slit in her panties and tights. Too bad the lunch rush was starting and people were starting to filter past her stall.

"I really want to make you come again," I murmured in her ear.

Her pale skin flushed. I kissed her then let her go.

While Lilith was busy with a customer selecting a hatpin, I looked around for my missing good luck charm.

Did I believe Lilith had murdered Patty? Not really, but there was evidence that could point to her. Then there was what had happened with her and Anna last night. Lilith was definitely hiding something from me. But it wasn't as if she was throwing herself at me as a distraction. In fact, she was being guarded.

You just want to get laid.

As soon as the teens left, I pulled Lilith back in for a kiss.

"Come on." I grabbed her hand. "You don't sell food; you don't get a ton of lunchtime traffic." I flipped her sign to Beware... I Will Return. "Let's go Christmas shopping."

"I do not have it in me to spend all afternoon shopping," she said.

"You're in luck," I told her, checking my watch, "because my shift starts in thirty minutes, and we're going to make your stall North Pole ready by then. If Ada doesn't come by today, then she will tomorrow. While you clearly know all things Halloween, you'll need a Christmas expert if you want to kill that citation."

Lilith flipped the sign back around. "Salem, you're in charge."

The black cat stood to attention and meowed at her.

"Seriously?" I asked.

"Salem knows how the shop is run."

Smokey was chewing on a stick Lilith had given him. He stood up when he saw me heading out.

"Stay," I told him, still not sure about leaving a cat in charge of a stall.

The Christmas market was gearing up for the lunch rush when we headed out.

"Is Salem really manning it?"

"If people want to pay cash, he can work the box," Lilith replied. "No one steals when he's there. Besides, you left Smokey. Between the two of them, they can manage." She smirked at me. "Now, Captain Christmas, Saint Nick me."

"There are three things you need for a good Christmas display. Well, maybe four. Candles."

"Already have those."

"Eh…" I waved my hand.

"I am not buying more candles." Lilith's tone was flat.

"Fine. Garland."

"I have garland," she said.

"Since when?"

"Since last night when I went into the woods and cut some."

"There is a murderer loose, Lilith, and you were just attacked."

"I've collected mushrooms in those woods since I was a little girl, and I'm not stopping now." She was defiant.

"Fine. You have garland, and I saw you have a tree already, which is item number three, though a Christmas tree covered in spiderwebs isn't exactly what Ada's expecting."

"The tree is fine," she argued. "It even has wrapped presents underneath it."

"Presents wrapped in black paper."

The stall we were passing had a barrel of glittering gold-and-red wrapping paper. I picked up a roll and took it to the counter.

"No."

"Yes. Look, the wrapping paper even says *Merry Christmas* on it."

"It's too bright. Can't we buy vintage wrapping paper, at least?" She held up a roll.

"No. Put that back. We want that nineties Christmas aesthetic."

Lilith grumbled as I bought the wrapping paper for her.

"Now, you need ornaments," I said as we headed back into the crowded market.

"I have ornaments," she insisted as I pulled her into a stall filled with a variety of ornaments.

"You need ornaments that scream *I love Christmas, and I'm not trying to poison people with my cat or my cookies.* These are so cool." I held up a glittering snowflake. While my excitement for Christmas knew no bounds, by the look on her face, I could tell that Lilith was not in the Christmas spirit.

"That doesn't go with my décor."

"Yes, it does because the ornaments are going everywhere, not just the tree."

She made a face.

"Think of your cookies and your citation," I said in a singsong. "Also, I just gave you the second-best orgasm of your life."

"Not feeling that sure of yourself?"

I kissed her then grinned against her mouth. "The best one is the one I'm giving you tonight. And I promise you will scream *Merry Christmas* when you come." I jingled a jolly Santa bell ornament at her.

"Fine." She sighed and grabbed a basket from the stall owner. "Ornament me."

"Don't be such a Grinch," I said as I filled the basket with ornaments. "Christmas is the most magical time of the year! Look at all the twinkling lights and the beautiful decorations. It's a time for love, joy, and spreading warmth." I set the basket at the sales counter.

"The credit card debt, the suppressed family drama that bubbles to the surface, the songs on repeat that make you want to claw your eardrums out," Lilith countered.

"So dramatic." I swiped my credit card.

"I can pay for it. It's my stall," Lilith protested.

"You're going to pay me back later, remember?" I winked at her.

We continued our trek through the market, sampling hot cocoa and gingerbread cookies that were foisted on us. I couldn't help stealing glances at Lilith. She looked beautiful in the soft glow of the holiday lights.

"This isn't a stroll through the Christmas market. This is a forced march," she complained as I added a festive vest for Salem to the pile of parcels.

"He is not going to wear that," Lilith warned me.

"He has to wear it," I reminded her. "He was part of the citation."

I left her with the packages for a moment then came back with two Christmas sandwiches. "You need to get your strength up."

"Why? Because you're going to give me a workout tonight?"

"Absolutely," I purred in her ear then took a bite of my oversize sandwich.

Lilith studied hers suspiciously. "Why is it oozing red?"

"I thought you were a goth girl." I tugged a lock of her hair. "This should be right up your alley. You're about to eat the famous Christmas sandwich. It's a culinary masterpiece, a harmonious blend of holiday flavors and textures that capture the essence of a festive feast between two slices of freshly baked artisan bread. It can also be repurposed as the

Thanksgiving sandwich. It all depends on how you brand it. Kind of like your shop."

She sniffed. "It smells like mashed potatoes."

"Hey, I had my mouth in your cunt. I think you can try this sandwich," I quipped.

Lilith's mouth dropped open. I stuck a corner of the sandwich between her lips. She took a bite, and her face lit up.

"Right?" I said, grinning at her. "Turkey, stuffing—yes, mashed potatoes—some green beans for color, and of course, cranberry relish to bring it all together."

Lilith took another huge bite.

"My mother dumped me at her uncle's place when I was a teenager, right after Thanksgiving. Uncle Don didn't know what to do with a teenage boy. He'd never had any kids, and I wasn't easy to get along with. I just hid in my room until he finally made me come out. We drove, like, an hour to here, the Harrogate Christmas Market. It wasn't as big as it is now. But this stall"—I inclined my chin toward the sandwich—"had the best thing I'd ever tasted."

I took another bite and sighed happily. "Perfection."

"I never really came to the Christmas market," Lilith said as I handed her a glass bottle of pomegranate-infused sparkling water. The little red seeds bounced in the bubbles.

"Christmas was too bright, too happy, too much of all my classmates going on and on about what their parents were going to buy them. I lived with my grandmother, and she was on a fixed income. The house was disintegrating around us, and she couldn't afford upkeep, let alone something like Christmas presents. She would always make us something for the holidays. She liked to knit. Or she'd fashion a present together out of old junk she'd found. I made the mistake when I was little of taking one of her dolls to school. The kids all freaked out and said it was creepy."

"Jeez."

"To be fair," Lilith said, pulling out her phone and swiping, "this is the doll in question."

"Damn," I said, staring at the horrifying doll on her phone screen. "Yeah, that could give someone nightmares."

"Anyway, then and there, I decided to embrace it. Christmas was dead to me. I was all in on Halloween."

"Until now." I elbowed her lightly.

"Christmas is better if you sell crafts." She wiped her hands and stood up, brushing the crumbs off her dress.

"Is Ada going to show up today? Did she say?" Lilith asked me as we headed back to her stall.

"She didn't answer when I called her, but if she does show up, text me, and I'll run over." I leaned in to kiss her. "I'll be back for the séance."

"Why?"

"If Heather thinks that one of the people at the séance is the murderer, then no way am I leaving you alone with them."

CHAPTER 22

I t had been tolerable to go to the Christmas market with Luke.

Actually, no. It had been more than tolerable. It had been fine.

Truthfully? It had been great.

I hummed along with the Christmas carols on the sound system as I strung up the pine boughs and, for some variation, interspersed them with mistletoe and juniper that I'd collected in the forest.

I loved decorating for Halloween. The day after Labor Day, my fall decorations were out. I left them up until Thanksgiving, just swapping a few of the spooky things out for a moody fall vibe.

Decorating for Christmas? Well, it wasn't so terrible. It was sort of nice to sit there, tying the garland and greeting people as they came in to shop. Solstice, after all, was a witchy festival, and the garland did smell nice.

I refused on principle to include the little Santa baubles in it. Instead, I was intertwining dried herbs, sticks of cinnamon, dried bits of citrus, and paper stars I cut out of that atrocious wrapping paper Luke had selected.

"Ooh!" one woman exclaimed, stopping to stare at my garland. "How much is that per yard?"

"It's not for—"

She whipped out a wad of cash. "I need a hundred feet of that. I have in-laws coming, and my husband's sister is not going to show me up this year." She set the cash down on the counter.

"I'll have it tonight. Tea for the holiday stress?" I offered.

"Yes, all of that, please."

Snow was falling fast, and it was dark outside by the time I'd finished the garland for my customer.

"You're so fast! Just in time too. My in-laws are coming into town tomorrow." She sniffed the curled-up garland in the box. "Smells so good, just like Christmas. Also, could I have more of that tea?"

"I had a feeling you might ask," I said, setting down a box with a neatly tied bow on the counter, then rang her up.

"Someone's getting into the Christmas spirit. I love the new setup," Anna said cheerfully as she passed the woman leaving with her parcels.

I'd hung the ornaments up against the black curtains. No, I did not take down my spiderwebs; it would have hurt my soul. I had interspersed the ornaments with bundles of dried oak leaves and some pine.

Anna snapped a photo. "I need you to come decorate my shop next year. The North Pole Nook is getting all the social media traffic, and she has a more cool-girl aesthetic like this."

"Seems like you've been busy with drink orders," I said, setting her order on the counter.

"Your spice blend is making them fly out the door on broomsticks." She giggled as I opened the box to show her the herbal contents.

Outside, thunder rumbled.

Salem startled and meowed.

"That's weird," Anna said nervously. "Usually, it doesn't thunder during snow."

"It's called thunder snow," I said. "Uncommon but possible."

Lightning flashed, and thunder sounded again, louder this time. The lights flickered.

"I guess I'd better get back before this storm gets any worse," Anna said.

Thunder clapped again, and the lights went out. Briefly lit from behind by the lightning refracted off thousands of snowflakes, a dark silhouette loomed in the doorway of the stall. Then Luke stepped inside, Smokey bounding in after him.

"Good evening, ladies."

The lights flickered as Luke leaned in to kiss me. "Bet you have an issue with the breaker. I'll take a look."

Anna grinned and shot me a thumbs-up. "Handsome and handy."

Behind the wall separating the sales counter from more storage space, Luke pulled open the little metal door of the breaker box. Clanging and clacking noises could be heard.

"I created another spice blend for you," I told Anna as I placed a little bag in her box and closed it. "Taste it, and give me your thoughts."

"Thanks!" Anna turned to leave and almost ran into Heather. "Excuse me."

Heather didn't move. "Not staying for the séance?"

The lights flickered again, and cold wind blew through the stall, extinguishing several of the candles.

Anna pressed her hand to her throat.

"We're trying to speak with Patty's ghost," Heather said, stepping into the stall. "Having more people there who knew her might help her to appear."

"There will be snacks," I told Anna.

"I suppose Ricky is here?" Heather asked. She seemed annoyed.

"I haven't seen him," Anna chirped.

Heather shot a death glare at Anna. "I wasn't talking to you. Where is Ricky, Lilith? Is he back there?"

Luke stepped out into the stall. "I think you need a new fuse. I'll bring one tomorrow."

"I have one at home I can use," I said.

Luke raised an eyebrow.

"I make sculptures with electrical components," I explained.

"Of course you do."

Heather relaxed, and her face brightened. "That's who you had hiding in here."

"They're a new item," Anna said.

Great. It was going to be all around town at this rate.

"Guess we better start planning the wedding," Heather gushed.

"And naming the baby," Anna quipped.

"I love baby clothes." Heather swooned. "I knit."

I ignored them and lit the candles.

Luke flicked off the lights. "Probably want to manage with candles for now just in case the wiring can't handle the strain."

"Perfect time for a séance," I said.

"Sit, Anna. Have some tea," Heather said.

"I don't want to intrude."

"I insist. Unless you have something to hide?" Heather laughed.

"What's so funny?" Ashley asked brightly from the door. She had another of her custom glittery scrunchies in her ponytail. This one was festooned with glittering glass baubles.

"Don't you have a curtain or something to put up, Lilith? The snow's getting inside," Heather complained.

"I'll get it," Luke offered, shaking out some black fabric.

"He really has made himself at home," Anna joked.

"I'm here. Guess we better see if Patty speaks to us," Ricky announced, ducking into the stall right as Luke began to hook up the curtain.

"Heather, Anna, Luke." Ricky slapped Luke on the shoulder. His gaze slid over Ashley then to me. "Nice outfit, Lilith. If you dressed like that in high school, I might have banged you. Right, Luke?" He elbowed the larger man.

Luke grabbed his arm and twisted it. "*The fuck did you say?*"

"Ricky! You're hurting him, Luke!" Ashley cried, rushing over, Heather behind her.

"That's my customer," I hissed at Luke, trying to pull him off. His hand was a vise on Ricky's arm.

Smokey growled.

Luke finally released Ricky with a shove.

"Fucking outsiders," Ricky muttered.

"Tea? Refreshments?" I asked then mouthed at Luke, "Stay in the corner."

His soft mouth was hard, his handsome face dangerous in the flickering light of the candles.

The group gathered around the square table I'd set out for the séance.

"You staying, Anna?" Ricky asked, rubbing his arm.

"Seems like Patty needs all the support she can get," Anna said wryly.

I lit a bundle of dried sage and wafted it, the smoke making patterns in the cold air. Then I took my seat.

A séance was all about the atmosphere, about putting people's minds and spirits into a state of receptiveness. Ignoring Luke's watchful gaze, I lit two candles on either side of Patty's portrait. Then I held out my hands, palms up.

"Join hands."

Anna tentatively placed hers in mine.

Ricky turned up his nose. "Aren't you supposed to have a—what's that thing? A Ouija board?"

"No, those are scams. Hands," I ordered.

Heather placed hers in mine and Ricky's.

I took a deep breath and closed my eyes, focusing my energy on the photograph before me. "Patty," I whispered, "if you can hear me, if your spirit lingers here, please come forward."

"But you have a board. I see it." Ricky pointed.

Heather grabbed his hand back.

"That's decoration," I snapped at him. "It's a Victorian antique. It doesn't work to communicate with the dead—too much user error. Also, the Victorians were hyped up on ether, opium, and rancid butter. They ran around hallucinating, board or no board. Patty, if you—"

"Do you offer refunds?" Ricky interrupted.

I ignored him.

"Patty?" I called loudly. "Are you with us, Patty?"

"Can you hear me now?" Ricky snickered.

A chilling breeze ran through the room, and the air felt charged with an otherworldly presence.

"We seek your guidance, Patty, to bring closure to those who knew you, and to shed light on the mysteries surrounding your life and death. Patty, if you have a message, if you wish to speak to those who remember you. Now is the time," I urged, my voice unwavering.

The room grew colder, and the photograph of Patty trembled on the table. Thunder clapped, and a chilling breeze blew past the curtains, bringing ice and snow into the stall.

The candle fluttered.

The photograph rattled and then toppled over, the glass breaking when it hit the floor. On the shelf, the various knickknacks rattled, and before I could catch them, several crashed to the floor.

"Oh my god! It's Patty!" Anna screamed.

"Patty, speak to us!" Ashley cried. "Tell us who murdered you!"

The shelf that held the letterpress that I used to create my custom signage toppled over, the little metal letters scattering everywhere.

"It's Patty." Ashley grabbed Ricky.

"I don't think so."

"No, it's Patty." She pointed at the floor.

Luke pulled out his flashlight, and it reflected off the metal letters that were arranged at Ricky's feet—by chance or by ghostly intervention? Who could say?

"It's a message from Patty," Ashley whispered.

THY R HEER

"Oh my god, oh my god!" Anna was hyperventilating and fanning herself. "Someone in this room is the murderer."

Ricky looked like he was about to throw up. "It's random chance. It's like statistics or whatever," he babbled, the whites of his eyes thick rings. "She can't be here, right? It's a trick, right? It was that cat."

"There are no tricks," I said in a clipped tone. "That was Patty, and she was angry."

"I can't... This is... I don't believe any of this." He abruptly ran out of the stall. The curtain caught on his coat, and he tore it down as he tried to get away.

"Tea?" I offered the rest of the women.

Heather pressed a trembling hand to her throat. "She's here?"

"Patty, can I have your Birkin bag, since you don't need it anymore?" Ashley asked to the ceiling.

"Are you fucking kidding me?" Luke mouthed.

The wind howled again, sending the letters tumbling. Luke flinched.

I pointed.

NOO.

"Dang." Ashley made a face.

I set water on to boil while Luke helped tidy up. After the kettle whistled, I poured the steaming, calming tea into mugs.

"Who do you think it is?" Ashley whispered after a moment.

"Someone in this room," I said.

"Or someone who just left," Luke added.

We looked at the doorway.

"He wouldn't... his own wife? Ricky loved her. She was his one true love," Anna insisted. "They were meant to be together. Homecoming king and queen." Anna's mouth turned down.

"That's a lie." Heather's voice was shrill. "Ricky's been having an affair."

"Bullshit!" Ashley yelled at her and jumped up.

"Why else would he act like that if he's not hiding something?" Anna asked.

"Who is he having an affair with?" I asked.

"I'm not sure," Heather said as she gathered her things. "Patty was concerned he was."

"What did she say exactly?"

"I don't know. I need to go home."

"And I need to get back to the shop," Anna said, grabbing her packages.

"Shouldn't we go find Ricky?" Ashley called, hurrying after them.

"Is that always how séances go?" Luke asked after a moment of silence.

"They're usually not that exciting," I said and finished picking up the last of the toppled display items. "An affair. I mean, I thought something was suspicious with Ricky. Maybe I should go back to his house and see if I can find out who it was. What if it's Anna? Though she wasn't really acting like they were together, not today anyway."

"Lilith." Luke cupped my face. "I didn't come here to look for clues. I came to convince you to come back to my place."

CHAPTER 23

His kisses were hot as we stumbled into one of the renovated industrial buildings off Main Street, where Luke lived.

Weathered leather sofas sat in the darkened living room, and dark wooden beams crisscrossed overhead. Industrial metal accents complemented worn leather-bound books, and vintage city maps and firefighting tools decorated the walls.

I didn't have time to register much more because he was pushing me down on that big leather couch.

"You gonna let me fuck you, Lilith?"

"Yeah, I—"

He pushed up my sweater, his large hands cupping my tits under my bra. I struggled to pull the sweater over my head as he kissed me all over, like he couldn't get enough of me.

Luke peeled off his shirt and threw it onto the hardwood floor.

I was still wearing the tights and panties he'd cut. He didn't bother trying to finesse his way around them, just pulled them down.

"My boots," I gasped.

My legs were tangled in the tights. He pushed the fabric down as far as it could go, then his fingers were playing in my slit, stroking me as I bucked against his hand. His mouth was on my tits, and his teeth grazed my nipple.

"I want to come all over your pussy," he growled at me as his fingers dipped into my opening, scissoring while I moaned and flexed around them.

All I wanted was his cock, to feel him huge inside me.

"I can't wait till you're coming on my cock," he rumbled.

Then I was coming on his hand. It was sudden—my body gave in, and I was shuddering on him.

He picked me up easily in his arms, kissed me as he carried me back to the bedroom, and threw me down on the bed face-first. He grabbed my ripped tights and pulled. With a loud tear, my legs were free. The panties were next.

Then he was on me—his mouth between my legs, one large hand grabbing my ass, holding me steady as he licked and sucked me, swirling his tongue around my clit. He forced my legs apart wider as I moaned, then his fingers were back in me, fucking me while his tongue worked my clit. I cried out as I came, and he milked the orgasm.

As I was catching my breath, I heard a condom packet rip.

Luke leaned over me, one hand tangled in my long hair, and growled, "Now that you're good and wet, I can fuck you just how I like, nice and hard."

"Yes," I moaned. "Please."

Hand on my ass, he used his other thumb to spread me wider. His cock poked at my opening.

"Take me," I mewled.

With no warning, he thrust into me hard. I cried out in pleasure as his cock filled me to the hilt. He grunted as he pulled out then took me again.

I panted as he thrust, whimpering as he filled me with that thick cock. I barely had a chance to get used to the huge length before he was fucking me. The buckle of his belt grazed my skin as he jackhammered into me. He hadn't even taken off all his clothes because he couldn't wait to fuck me.

Suddenly, it was too much. I crested over the edge and came with a cry, but he wasn't done with me. He kept up the furious pace until I thought I was going to pass out, panting and clawing at the bedcovers. Too soon, he was coming inside me with a grunt.

"*Fuck.*"

"You really are Captain Christmas," I panted as he collapsed next to me. I reached out to run my black nails through his blond hair.

He kicked off his pants, and I unzipped my boots then tossed them to the floor.

Luke wrapped those huge muscular arms around me. "You're so fucking beautiful."

"I see why people want a boyfriend," I mumbled sleepily.

His breathing steadied. Outside, snow fell.

I think I might actually like Christmas.

Distantly, I heard a soft ping.

Then another one.

My phone.

I could ignore it, but maybe it was Morticia or Penny. Anna's getting attacked had me on edge. What if they needed me?

Slowly, so I didn't disturb Luke, I slid from under his arm and padded into the living room. My phone was on the floor next to my sweater dress, glowing with several text messages:

Winston Girthman: *Okay, just sent you the scanned report.*
Winston Girthman: *We're even, right?*
Winston Girthman: *Right, Lilith????*
Lilith: *Yes.*

I opened the attachments and sat down on the couch to read the report. Salem had curled up next to Smokey in his basket, and he purred as he kneaded the dog's head.

The autopsy report included diagrams and a write-up about the findings of the big-city coroner. I scrolled through the PDF to the cause-of-death section.

Evidence of stab wounds, 1mm–4mm size melted glass found in wounds. While blood was found in the wounds, it is likely that wounds were caused postmortem, ostensibly by a sharp falling object. Cause of death was blunt force head trauma.

I sat back on the sofa, barely able to breathe.

Good news: Morticia was definitely not the murderer, and we could prove it.

Bad news: someone had murdered Patty, either in my stall or outside, then dragged her in and set the fire.

Worse news: Luke had lied to me.

I didn't know what to think. Why had Luke lied? Did he know about the report? He must know, right?

I tiptoed back into the bedroom, but the large firefighter was fast asleep.

I debated waking him up. A car drove past, and the headlights briefly illuminated the wall opposite the bed. On it hung more firefighting paraphernalia, including what appeared to be a harness with very familiar-looking buckles.

Goddess, save me.

I clenched my jaw so I wouldn't make a sound.

Luke was the murderer.

And I had slept with him

As I crept across the bedroom, the old wood floor creaked as I reached for my boots. I froze as Luke stirred. Then he went back to sleep

I only let out my breath when I was back in the living room. Not bothering to put on my bra, I threw the sweaterdress over my head, grabbed my purse, and tiptoed to the door.

I bit back a yelp.

By the door was an axe, a big one, with a handle that you could kill someone with.

"Salem," I whispered to the cat.

His ears flicked up, and his yellow eyes narrowed.

"Come," I mouthed and waved to him.

The cat slowly roused himself while I stuffed my feet into my boots and snatched my jacket off the floor.

Luke had been complaining about not having enough excitement in Harrogate, I reminded myself as I took the stairs out of his building two at a time. He'd been entranced by fire, almost addicted to the candles I had out. The buckle was his. Maybe he had started the fire so he could be the town hero. He was an outsider. Maybe he just wanted to fit in.

Salem hung on to my coat for dear life as I ran away from the building.

Had Patty seen him starting the fire, so he'd killed her? Now that he knew I was on the trail, he'd thrown obstacles in my way, distracted me, and fed me false information.

When I was several blocks away, I slowed down enough to take out my phone.

Lilith: *Meet me tomorrow morning. I think I've solved the murder.*

CHAPTER 24

hadn't been able to sleep at all that night. Instead, I'd stood by the door of my studio garage apartment, waiting and wondering if Luke was going to realize that I knew he was the murderer and come kill me.

Salem, picking up on my anxiety, paced by the window and hissed any time the wind knocked the branches against the glass.

I had finished my fourth cup of black tea when I walked up to Anna's café after checking on my stall. Inside, it was warm and smelled like cinnamon. Christmas carols played softly on the sound system.

I was not in the mood.

I ordered another black tea for me and coffee for Penny along with pastries and an herbal tea for Morticia then grabbed a table. I was too anxious to eat anything, and I spun the cup around on the table. I jumped when my phone buzzed with another call from Luke.

I sent it to voicemail.

Maybe I should answer him with some sort of explanation. Or maybe it was too late, and he was already suspicious.

"Why is it so early?" Penny yawned and pulled out a chair.

"It's ten," I snapped at Penny.

"Yikes. Someone needs to get laid."

"That's the problem. I already did! I shouldn't have been thinking like a horny teenager. That's why I missed the obvious signs." I groaned.

Penny's mouth opened and closed like a guppy's. "You—"

"What did you miss, Lilith?" my twin asked, taking the chair next to me. She selected one of the cinnamon buns and took a bite.

"I solved it. I solved the murder," I said then explained in a low voice what I'd discovered about Luke.

"He seems so nice," Penny said in shock. "Those blue eyes. That hair."

"You never know," Morticia said.

"Maybe you're wrong," Penny commented.

"No, I'm sure I know who the murderer is," I insisted. "There is only one obvious conclusion. I'm going to the police this afternoon, so hopefully at least the chief of police will be involved, and I won't have to deal with the incompetent officers."

I stuffed the buckle into Penny's purse. "Hide this somewhere safe," I ordered her. "Right now, it's our only piece of evidence."

I drained my tea, and Morticia packed up the pastries to go.

"Please go straight home," I told them as we stood outside. "You two need to stay safe. The murderer is clearly escalating."

I hugged my friends.

"So dramatic." Morticia sighed.

"You have to believe me," I argued.

"You should consult the cards before you throw the man to the wolves," my twin suggested sagely.

"Yeah, this is your only chance for a boyfriend." Penny grimaced.

Trudging back through the snow to my stall—I'd left Salem in charge, but the lunch rush was gearing up—I wondered what I should do. Not that I was going to get back with Luke. Despite what Penny had said, I knew I was right. I didn't need to lay out any cards or read tea leaves to know. All the evidence pointed to him.

Well, not all of it. A single piece of real evidence and then some circumstantial evidence. Did I have enough to go to the cops?

My phone rang in my bag. I pulled it out and hit the red button to end the call.

Luke: *We need to talk. Can I come see you?*

No, I wasn't talking to him!

The Christmas market wasn't too crowded yet, and the mass of tourists thinned out the closer I got to my stall.

The phone rang again.

What if Luke showed up? What was I going to do? Maybe I needed to leave town. I'd go to the police, and then I'd leave.

What about my art, my livelihood?

Behind me, I heard heavy boots. Was it Luke?

I took off at a jog toward my stall. The air smelled like Christmas trees, sugar cookies, and a cheerful, burning Yule log.

Wait. Burning? *Fire?*

"Oh my god, Lilith!" David sprinted up to me. "Your stall's on fire! I called the fire department."

I dropped my bag. "Salem's in there. Did you see Salem? Did you see my cat? He's black."

"No, but the fire department's coming. They'll find him."

"I told him to stay in the stall! Salem!" I screamed, but the cat didn't appear. "He's in the stall. He has to be."

Wrapping my scarf around my mouth, I raced toward the flames.

"*Salem!*"

CHAPTER 25
Luke

Why the hell had she left?

And why the hell was she ignoring all my messages?

I would go to her stall, but as soon as I'd gotten in to work, we had to load up the truck to deal with a mobility scooter pileup.

I spent the next several hours treating irate seniors and calling their kids.

"Shoot me before I ever get that old and crazy." Cliff groaned as we parked the truck inside the station garage.

"Uh-huh," I said, checking my phone for the thousandth time, hoping Lilith had responded.

"Ooh, did someone finally get a girlfriend?"

"Fuck off."

Why had she just disappeared in the middle of the night? I would say I had dreamt the whole thing, but she'd left her tights and panties in my bedroom.

The alarm rang.

"It's a fire!" Eddie bellowed as the dispatcher's voice squawked on the speaker. "A real one."

Grabbing my gear, I jumped back into the truck. Cliff flicked on the lights and sirens, and we raced down Main Street.

"Weren't we just here?" Eddie asked as the truck jerked to a halt at a familiar corner of the Christmas market.

I didn't answer.

Smokey whined and scratched at the truck door.

"Fuck. *No*."

Lilith's stall was engulfed in flames.

"She's not in there. She can't be in there." I threw open the truck door.

Smokey sprang out, galloping headlong toward the fire. I tried to call the dog back, but he ignored me. I raced after him and slid to a stop in front of the burning stall.

David screamed and pointed at the raging inferno. "*Lilith!*"

I briefly checked my mask then stepped into the fire.

Or tried to. One of Lilith's bookcases had toppled over in front of the exit, probably the reason she was trapped in there.

Hefting my axe, I hacked the bookcase into pieces. The inside of the stall was dark. Between the black curtains and the smoke, I could barely see anything.

Crouching, I felt around on the ground. My gloved hand connected with something that felt like an arm. Squinting in the thick black smoke, I could barely make out a prone form. I grabbed Lilith around her waist and sprinted out of the shed then threw her onto the ground a few paces away.

Townspeople crowded around us.

"Oxygen." Cliff set the canister next to me.

"Is she dead?"

"Who is that?"

"Is that Lilith?"

"And after someone just killed Patty."

"Guess we know it wasn't Lilith."

The crowd took photos and livestreamed the tragedy.

"Damn rubberneckers," I muttered as I held the clear plastic mask to Lilith's mouth and nose.

"Anyone else in there?" Cliff asked.

I shook my head.

"She's dead, isn't she?"

"I don't think she's dead."

"Get back!" I barked at the onlookers.

"Where is Smokey? He's supposed to be doing crowd control," I demanded over the wailing sirens and the roar of the fire hose.

Lilith's normally pale skin was ghostly white.

"Where's the ambulance?"

Cliff dumped a handful of snow onto Lilith's face. She sat up, fists flying. Cliff cursed as Lilith stumbled to her feet. I ducked her fist and reached for her.

"Get off me! Salem! *Salem!* I need to rescue Salem!"

I grabbed her around the waist, forcing her back to the ground with a grunt before she could sprint headlong into the burning stall.

"You can't go back in there," I said as she sobbed on my shoulder.

"Salem's in there! Let me go!" she screamed, tearing at my heavy protective clothing. She sobbed as the fire was extinguished and the shed collapsed into a wet, steaming heap of wood.

"*No!*" Lilith wailed.

"I'm so sorry," I whispered to her as I stroked her back. "I'm so sorry."

"Smokey, you're falling down on the job," Cliff said behind me.

The big Dalmatian appeared next to me, a limp black scrap of fur in his mouth.

"Oh shit!" Eddie yelled. "Where's the pet mask?"

"Salem!" Lilith cried, grabbing her cat from Smokey and crushing him to her chest.

"Let him get some air." I grabbed her wrist.

Smokey licked Salem's head as I held the mask to his snout and turned up the oxygen.

Lilith cradled the cat, petting him gently. He made a wheezing noise then sneezed.

"Salem, you're alive." Tears streaming down her face, Lilith snuggled the cat, his furry head soaking up her tears.

I stroked her face, the heavy gloves catching on the strands of her dark hair.

"Let me check you out," I told her, grabbing the medic kit. I checked her vital signs while Salem got another of his nine lives plugged in.

Smokey was doing his best to keep the crowd away, but the entire mass of Christmas market shoppers must have been packed into this tiny out-of-the-way corner. He barked angrily.

I looked up. "*You.*"

Across from me stood Ricky, looking mildly nauseous and antsy.

He had been acting suspicious at the séance last night. Now, he thought Lilith was onto him, and he'd come back to finish her.

I knew it.

"What the fuck did you *do*, Ricky?" I roared, jumping to my feet. "You started the fire! I know you did! You tried to kill my girlfriend!"

There were screams from the crowd.

"Luke, Jesus, stop it. Stop!" Cliff yelled. He and Eddie each grabbed one of my arms as I threw myself at Ricky.

"You did this! I'm going to kill you!" I bellowed.

"*Dude*," Cliff yelled.

Ricky took off sprinting. Smokey started to chase him.

Cliff whistled. "Smokey, no!"

Smokey stood a few paces away from me, hackles raised, teeth exposed. I strained against my friends' hold.

"Luke, you can't go after him. You good?" Eddie smacked the top of my helmet. "You good?"

"Yeah, I'm good."

Next to me, Lilith's whole body was shaking. Her dark eyes were wide.

"Go take care of your girl," Cliff ordered. "Go."

CHAPTER 26

Dizzy. I felt so dizzy as Luke helped me into his apartment.

I'm back in the murderer's lair. He brought me here to kill me.

Luke had started the fire, right? He knew that I knew that he was a murderer and had tried to kill Salem. Now he was going to finish us both off.

Wrenching out of Luke's grasp, I grabbed one of the heavy antique fire axes off the wall and swung it at him.

"What the fuck!" Luke dove behind the couch.

Smokey yelped, and Salem hissed at me.

"You tried to kill me," I gasped. My arms were trembling, I was annoyed to find. I did metalworking. Why had I turned so weak all of a sudden?

Oh right, I'd almost died.

Thanks a fucking lot, Luke.

"I have evidence."

"Lilith." He held out a hand. "Put that axe down."

"Admit it!" I yelled at him. "Admit you killed Patty and tried to kill me and Salem." I swung the axe threateningly but accidentally lost control and smashed a lamp.

"Lilith, what the fuck? I didn't kill Patty, and I certainly didn't try to kill you. I would never hurt you!" Luke shouted. "I love you, and I don't want to lose you." His blue eyes were so sincere.

I was immune. "I don't believe you. I have evidence."

"You don't..." He was incredulous. "You literally don't have any evidence because I didn't do anything. The smoke has gone to your brain. Sit down, and let me get you some tea and soup."

"So you can *poison* me?" I screeched.

"God help me."

"I found your buckle in the fire," I spat.

His jaw dropped as he cut the innocent-hero act.

Got you.

"Wait. You found my buckle?" he asked, advancing on me.

"Yes," I said, hefting the axe. "Don't even try to kill me so you can take it back because it's in a safe place. If I go missing, my friend is going to the police."

"Lilith," Luke said slowly, "that's my lucky charm. I must have lost it in the fire when I was trying to save Patty, not because I killed her. I was at the fire station all day that day. I didn't leave until we got the alarm. You can pull the security footage from any of the cameras around the station. Or ask Cliff. Shoot, ask the chief."

"Liar!" I screeched. "I saw the report. You lied to me. You said she was stabbed, but she wasn't."

"Yes, she was," Luke said slowly. "Cliff told me."

"I have a copy of the report," I snarled.

Luke took two steps back then pulled his phone out of the pocket.

My arms trembled from holding up the heavy axe. I just wanted to lie down.

"Hey, Cliff? Yeah, she's fine. Tried to chop my head off... What? Never mind. The autopsy report. I thought you said it said that Patty was stabbed... Uh-huh... Okay, what did it actually say? You didn't get a copy? Apparently, he didn't get a copy," Luke told me. "I mean you passed on bad information, man. Patty was killed by blunt force trauma. Yeah, Bobby is a moron. You think he knows how to read an autopsy report?"

Luke hung up the phone. "So, yeah, apparently the stabbing was hearsay," he said, sitting down in a chair a few feet from me.

Salem jumped into his lap.

"Traitor," I hissed at the cat.

Salem rolled over and purred as Luke stroked his tummy.

"He seems to have cashed in his latest life. Lilith thought you were a goner, boy."

The cat meowed.

"I know. She doesn't have any faith in me either."

"But the evidence..." I protested. The evidence that was looking weaker by the minute.

Just like my arms.

"Why don't you have something to eat while you sift through hours of mind-numbing security footage?" Luke offered.

Giving up, I dropped the axe and collapsed onto the couch. Luke set his laptop in front of me.

"Maybe you're just trying to throw me off the trail," I croaked.

"Or maybe I'm trying to convince you to drop it so that we can find the real murderer, who is Ricky, by the way. I'm convinced. He was your first suspect, right?"

Luke hit a button, and silent security footage played.

"Are you guys playing a board game?" I peered at the screen.

"There are only so many times you can scrub a floor," he said, standing up and heading to the kitchen area, which opened into the living room.

I checked the time stamp on the video. That was the time of the murder.

Leaning my head back and closing my eyes, I wondered how I could have been so wrong. Luke had an alibi.

I opened my eyes when he set a tray with soup, tea, and toast in front of me.

"You made soup?" I asked Luke weakly as he draped a blanket over me.

"Minestrone."

He held up the bowl for me. After a few bites of the hearty soup, I was feeling better.

"When I was trying to find Salem, I thought I heard someone walking around outside, like someone in heavy boots. But maybe it was just the stall collapsing."

"Or maybe it was the murderer," Luke replied seriously.

I'd come dangerously close to dying. It was chilling, and not in a fun way, to think that if Luke hadn't saved me, I'd be a goner just like Patty.

Luke's eyes narrowed. "At the fire today, Ricky was hovering around, acting strange. I bet it was him."

"It is always the husband."

"Usually a good place to start," Luke agreed, picking up a pen and paper from the coffee table. He started a numbered list. "Motive: Ricky has the life insurance payout."

"Heather thinks he was having an affair, which is also motive," I added. "Ricky kills Patty so he and his side chick can live happily ever after on the money."

"How does the blackmail fit into it?" Luke asked.

"It doesn't," I admitted, "but not all the clues have to be related. This isn't a movie. In real life, the husband kills his wife for money or jealousy, and he doesn't do that good of a job covering his tracks."

"How did he kill her?"

"Cause of death is blunt force trauma. There were lots of things in my storage shed that could have killed her."

Luke wrote a question mark. "Why would Ricky and Patty be in the shed?"

I tapped my chin. "Maybe Patty caught him with his affair partner, and they argued."

"We'd need to find video evidence that Ricky was with Patty at the Christmas market."

"We will, but first," I said after scooping down the last of the soup, "we need to go back to my stall. I bet Ricky left a clue there."

"Lilith, please stay and rest." Luke took my hand. "I meant what I said. I love you." He leaned in to kiss me. "You smell like smoke."

"You can't love me. You don't even know me," I argued.

Luke smiled at me softly. "You ran into a burning building to save your beloved pet, which sounds like a girl after my own heart. I love you. I can't lose you."

"I—" I hesitated.

His face was so open, so honest.

I did believe he was in love with me. I wasn't ready to say it back, though.

I stroked his cheek, and he leaned into my hand.

"Fine." He kissed me one more time. "You can have fifteen minutes. You have to wear my coat and scarf, and then you have to promise me that you'll let me take you back here so you can rest."

CHAPTER 27

"Tell me if you see anyone I know," I told Luke, half hiding behind him as we walked through the Christmas market.

Luke turned to me, grinning. "You look cute."

He'd made me wear one of his bright-red fleece-lined firemen coats, which was decorated with reflective strips. He'd stuck one of those fleece hunting caps with the earflaps on my head and wrapped a bright-green scarf with reindeer on it around my neck.

"Why do you even own a scarf like this?" I complained.

"One of the local senior citizens gifted me that scarf after I saved her Oldsmobile from her snowed-in driveway," he explained, his voice tinged with mirth. "It was handmade with love."

He adjusted the scarf around my neck and leaned in to kiss me slowly, like he could have spent all afternoon there with his arms around me.

Luke took my gloved hand in his and led me toward my ruined stall. The smell of burnt wood and all the herbs that had gone up in flames hung in the winter air, pungent and acrid as we approached through one of the back alleyways.

"Now, stay behind me," Luke warned me. "If you see something, I will grab it, not you. I don't want the stall to collapse on you."

"I'm not going inside."

"I know, but"—he clasped his other hand around mine—"I just can't lose you."

As we approached the corner of the market where my stall was—we couldn't see it but could smell it—we passed behind the Christmas committee help-desk stalls. In the shadows, two figures were locked in a passionate embrace. They probably assumed no one would be able to see them and that they were safe for the moment.

Luke made a noise of surprise.

The man jumped and turned.

"Ricky," Luke spat out.

"Shit!" Ricky tried to disentangle himself from a woman wearing a fancy Chanel snowsuit.

Smokey growled and took off after Ricky. He boxed him in so he couldn't flee.

Luke sprinted over, grabbed him by the collar, and slammed him into the wooden wall on the back side of the stall.

Ricky screamed and tried to push Luke off.

Though the men were the same height, Ricky's high school football days were long behind him, whereas Luke worked out regularly and had a physically demanding job.

"Help! He's going to kill me! Help!"

Luke socked him in the stomach. Ricky doubled over.

"Lilith, call off your brute!" Ashley shrieked at me.

Yes, *Ashley*.

"You're the one he was cheating on Patty with," I said.

"I wasn't cheating. I was faithful," Ricky wheezed. "Ashley and I only just started hooking up. I swear it."

"I don't believe it."

"Did you help kill her too?" I asked Ashley.

"What? I didn't kill Patty. We were friends."

"You hated that bitch," Ricky argued.

Luke punched him again. "Watch your language. That's your dead wife."

"She was horrible to me," Ricky ground out, collapsing on the ground at Luke's feet.

"Motive," I said.

"Not motive," Ricky whined. "I don't have it in me to kill anyone. You always said I was a spineless twit. Right, Lilith?"

"Then it had to be you," I said to Ashley. "Patty was found with bits of melted glass in her wounds. Glass…" I reached up to flick the custom-decorated scrunchie with mini Christmas ornaments in her hair. "Like that."

Ashley gasped and reached up to clasp her head. "You can't think I killed her."

"You have means, motive, and opportunity," I told her.

"My scrunchie broke. The silver twine I used was some cheap crap. It broke the morning of the murder after we gave you the citation. It snagged on a wreath in a Christmas market stall while Heather and I were doing a cookie-baking demonstration. I did a whole TikTok video on how to fix it," she said, pulling out her phone to show me.

"Hmm," I said, studying the scrunchie on the screen. "Still doesn't change the fact that you and Ricky were having an affair."

She looked at Ricky with guilt.

"Don't," Ricky said. "I'll be ruined."

"Grow up," Ashley snapped at him. "Yes, we were having an affair before Patty… died. But she was horrible to Ricky. Withholding sex—"

"Patty wanted me to work out more. Said I was an embarrassment," Ricky whined.

"You're a handsome Santa Claus." Ashley made a kissy-face at him.

"But that means we have an alibi," Ricky said, holding up a hand and pulling his phone out of his pocket. "I have proof we were together when your storage shed burned down."

He tapped his phone, and up popped a homemade porn video, his flabby, flat buttocks pounding away in an unoccupied Christmas stall.

"Please, no." I held up my hand in front of the screen.

"No, look," he insisted. "See the time stamp and the location?"

"Why were you making a sex tape in the middle of the Christmas market?" Luke asked in disgust.

On the screen, Ashley let out a loud cry, and a ceramic elf toppled off a shelf.

It probably committed suicide.

"I guess you're innocent," I said begrudgingly.

"We're going to live happily ever after!" Ashley threw herself into Ricky's arms and kissed him passionately.

I followed Luke down the alley.

"Guess we don't really need to look at the stall," Luke said, "since Ricky was a big dead end."

"It wasn't that big."

Luke laughed and nudged me lightly with his elbow.

"Who else is on your suspect list?" he asked me as we stood a few paces back and inspected the blackened, ruined heap of my livelihood.

"Not Anna. I thought Ricky might be having an affair with her, and she would be motivated enough to kill Patty, but apparently, the affair was with Ashley. And you're clear."

He gave me a quick kiss. "Of course I am."

"My sister didn't do it." I sighed. "We need to follow up on the blackmail angle. Whoever Patty sent the note to is currently the number-one suspect."

Luke wrapped an arm around me, tucking me close to his warm body. "We can investigate from home, where it's not freezing."

I picked up Salem and tucked him into the coat.

Luke rested his chin briefly on my head. "Or you could just let the police handle it. Now that your stall burned down, no one in town thinks you did it."

"Maybe."

"I can show you how much I was worried about you," he said, cupping my face, then kissed me.

I wasn't ready to give up. I felt like I was close to solving the mystery.

Inside Luke's apartment, it was toasty. Outside the large steel-frame windows, snow fell, coating the rooftops nearby in a blanket of white.

"I need to find a Christmas tree," Luke said from the kitchen. "Maybe we can go tomorrow."

Was it weird how much he had just integrated me into his life? Maybe, but then it also felt nice to be wanted.

"I am not going to be working the Christmas market, so why not buy a tree?" I said, opening up his laptop.

"I like to go to the woods and cut one."

"Of course you do," I said, navigating through the folders of videos to pull security-camera footage from the day of Patty's death. The cameras closest to my stall had all been blacked out, thanks to David, but what about the ones near the Christmas committee stall?

"You're supposed to be resting," Luke reminded me, setting down a mug of tea.

"I want to check the security footage," I explained, pulling him down for a kiss.

He was nice to kiss. Maybe this wouldn't be such a bad Christmas after all.

"At least you don't have to put on a whole Christmas pageant for Ada," Luke reminded me as he headed back to the kitchen.

I scanned through the videos as Luke warmed up more soup.

There was Patty in her matching Chanel snowsuit. She was heading to the Christmas committee stall. A few moments later, an older man with a mustache followed her and grabbed her arm.

It looked like they were arguing. The man was angry and gesturing.

Behind me, the soup bubbled on the stove.

In the video, bits of light glinted on the screen, obscuring what was happening. I rewound the video, watched, then rewound it again. What was that light from?

"Find anything?" Luke called as dishes clanked.

Patty turned.

The glints were coming from a scrunchie. She had a scrunchie on her wrist—the one Ashley had made her. The one with glass baubles.

I quickly flipped to the autopsy report. There was no mention of it in her personal effects. That meant the murderer took it.

And I was looking right at him.

"Do you almost have your energy back?" Luke came over with a tray of more soup.

I quickly closed the laptop and said, "I think I'm done with investigating for the day."

Because how could I tell Luke that his beloved uncle, the fire chief, was the murderer?

CHAPTER 28

Luke

Lilith seemed on edge as she ate her soup.

"Are you worried I'm going to eat you up?" I asked her with a crooked smile. "Because I'm not. I'm just going to eat you out."

She didn't smile back. Her eyes flicked to the laptop then back to her soup.

"You found something," I said flatly.

Lilith didn't answer.

"You know who the murderer is."

She set her half-eaten soup aside and gave me an almost-sad look. "I believe so."

"What? What aren't you telling me? Lilith, who is it?" I jumped up and grabbed her shoulders.

Lilith opened up the laptop, navigated to a video, and then clicked Play.

We watched silently as the fire chief left city hall. Lilith went to another camera. There he was walking through the Christmas market. In another clip, he and Patty were arguing.

"You can't believe my uncle killed Patty," I choked out. "He has no reason to. He's a firefighter. He saves people. He doesn't hurt them."

Next to Lilith, Salem puffed up, agitated.

Lilith, voice aggravatingly calm, said, "We know Patty was blackmailing someone related to an adoption record or rumor she dug up. For a while, I assumed she was targeting one of the other girls we went to high school with. However, you and your great uncle are outsiders in this town. And your uncle is popular with the public servants. Patty is—was—vying for the mayoral title. What better way than to have the popular fire chief endorse you? He was her secret weapon that she mentioned on the white board in Heather's house. This video proves it. We see them arguing. What else would make your uncle angrily confront someone in broad daylight like that?"

I took a shaky breath. "My uncle is not a murderer."

"Maybe we should go to the fire station."

"The chief around?" I asked Cliff when I stomped into the fire station.

"Nope, but we saved Smokey a bone! The mayor sent over food."

"It was a huge barbeque spread," Eddie said and tossed Smokey his treat.

"I'm surprised you can even fit into the truck," Cliff joked.

"I ate your share because you weren't here, Luke." Eddie laughed.

"I saved you some. Don't worry," Cliff assured me.

"Uh-huh."

Cliff jumped up when he saw the dark expression on my face. "What happened?" His attention shifted to Lilith. "You should be resting."

"I'm trying to solve a murder," she replied.

Smokey settled down on the floor next to me, chewing his bone. Salem prowled around the wheels of the truck, probably looking for mice.

"Have you noticed the chief acting... weird lately?" I asked hesitantly.

My friends shrugged.

"You would know better than we do," Cliff said.

My jaw clenched. Uncle Don *had* been acting weird. He'd tried to steer me away from investigating the murder, he'd told me to keep my head down, and he'd been cagey and jumpy. Maybe he really was the murderer.

Lilith butted in. "I have reason to believe your fire chief murdered Patty because she was trying to blackmail him about an adopted child. How well do you know Chief Reynolds?"

In shock, Eddie and Cliff looked at each other then at me.

"What the hell, dude?" Eddie demanded.

"He tried to kill me. More importantly, he almost killed my cat." Lilith's dark eyes were unblinking. "I want my pound of flesh."

I felt sick thinking about the chief being the murderer.

"He didn't come around today," Cliff said slowly. "Which is odd."

"You know how last time he was around after the fire?" Eddie added. "This time, he didn't come do a report or anything after the stall burned down."

"One of you, go get the police," Lilith ordered. "We're going to city hall. He might be hiding in his office or about to skip town."

Cliff saluted.

"Salem, let's go," Lilith called.

The cat didn't show up.

"Cliff, have you seen Salem?"

"We can check the cameras," Cliff offered.

We followed him to the server room. Cliff opened up the security video files and rewound to ten minutes ago. There was the fire chief, my uncle, the man who had taken me in.

He walked up the path to the station and paused. He must have heard us. A black shadow crept along the ground then recoiled as the chief reached for him, picking up Salem by the scruff of his neck.

Lilith hissed in an angry breath.

The chief seemed angry as he tucked the struggling cat under his arm.

Cliff paused the video, shock written on his face. "The chief kidnapped Salem."

"No." I closed my eyes. "No, he can't be the murderer."

Cliff rested a hand on my shoulder. Lilith turned on her heel and headed back out into the garage space.

"I'll get the police. It will be easier to just go over there than to try to call dispatch," Cliff said as he shrugged on his coat.

"I'm going to kill him, and you all are going to see what a crime scene really looks like." On her way out, Lilith picked up one of the axes hanging on the wall.

"Just let me talk to him first," I begged, taking the axe from her. "It might just be a big misunderstanding."

But I knew in my heart it wasn't.

The sun was setting as we headed to city hall. My uncle's office was on the third floor. It was dark and empty. I flicked on a light, my hand on the axe.

Lilith didn't seem apprehensive. She immediately went to his desk and started pulling out drawers, looking for hidden clues.

"Found it." She held up a familiar letter.

Her phone beeped, and she read the message out loud.

"I have your cat. Come to city hall. The clock tower. Come alone." She slipped the phone back into her pocket. "How dramatic."

"Fuck." I sagged.

"What's the area code?"

"It's 838."

"Damn. That's the area code of our old town where we used to live before my uncle landed this job in Harrogate."

Lilith was already gone.

"Please, Lilith," I begged as she glided to the stairwell, looking less like a scared young woman wanting to rescue her cat and more like a dangerous vampire risen from the dead to enact her revenge on unsuspecting townspeople. "He's my only family. Just let me talk to him first."

"He has my cat. Salem is my family. No one touches my family." She marched up the stairs to the clock tower. "But," she said as we paused in the vestibule, "I do seem to be enamored with you, so you may have five minutes with him. That is all."

CHAPTER 29

"I love you," Luke said desperately. He briefly rested his forehead against mine then opened the oversize solid-wood door that led into the round room of the clock tower. Before he shut it behind him, I heard a faint meow from Salem.

I almost called the whole thing off and told Luke that I was just going to go in there and attack his uncle myself. Instead, I set my watch. I had texted Morticia and Penny for reinforcements. Not that Penny would be much use, but Morticia certainly had no problem pulling out fingernails.

I must really like Luke or something if I was going to let him try to talk his uncle down from the ledge.

It wasn't an actual ledge, of course. This clock tower wasn't a gothic tower—it was a nice space that people rented out for baby showers or wedding receptions. It was also a popular tourist spot because it was the highest point in town and offered a nice view from the large windows. During nice weather, you could see the Manhattan skyline.

In the vestibule next to me was the shrine to Patty, displaying candles, a ceramic cup stylized to look like a to-go coffee cup with PSL written on it, and personal effects, including Patty's yearbook.

Picking up the yearbook, I wondered if the chief's surprise daughter had gone to high school with me and Patty. Why would the chief kill over the information, though? Was he trying to run for a government position and thought this would ruin his chances?

I flipped open the yearbook, wondering if Patty had made any additional notes. The book opened to the photo of Ricky with his trophy.

"That's... weird." The photo, when I'd seen it in her house, had hearts all over Ricky's photo and sloppy romantic messages. This had nothing.

I thumbed through the yearbook, thinking it was a different photo or maybe someone else's yearbook. But there was Patty's custom nameplate that her dad had let her design back before you could just print these things off the internet. She had put them in every single book or item she owned.

Property of Patty Harrison.

"What the hell?"

Suddenly, I knew. I was wrong—the chief wasn't the murderer. Heather was. That was Heather's writing in the yearbook we'd seen in Patty's bedroom. Heather was in love with Ricky—maybe they had been having an affair and she wanted to get rid of Patty. All the girls thought Ricky was hot in high school. Heather might never have gotten over that teenage infatuation.

She killed Patty with that rolling pin, and the glass was from her scrunchie. She must have stolen Patty's to keep suspicion off her.

I set the book down quietly, grabbed the cup for a projectile weapon, then eased the door open.

I was hit by the noxious smell of gasoline.

Across the ornate room, Luke was on the floor next to the chief with his hands above his head. They were both soaked in gasoline.

Heather held Salem, who was wrapped in a gasoline-soaked towel, under her arm. In her other hand, she held her phone and a lighter.

Luke made eye contact with me and subtly shook his head.

Heather caught the motion and whirled around.

"Lilith, I was just texting you. It's almost as if you're a witch who can see the future." Heather laughed.

Salem meowed pitifully.

"Put my cat down."

"I know you're a fraud. Your little stunt with the séance was because you were onto me. You were trying to out me as a murderer. That's why I had to burn down your stall," Heather spat. "But you just wouldn't die."

"I can't believe you killed Patty over a boy. Over Ricky, no less. Don't you have any goddamn self-respect?" I asked, taking a step toward her.

"You were after him too! Everyone was after him!" Heather shrieked at me. "Ricky was mine. He was in love with me. Patty treated him like shit. She was such a nag. I took care of him. I cooked all his favorite foods. I bought him shirts. He was going to leave her to be with me, but then he stopped returning my calls." Heather started sobbing. "She stole him from me."

"Actually," I said, "she didn't. Ashley stole him."

"That hussy!" Heather screeched. "Every girl in this town is a boyfriend-stealing skank—Ashley, Anna, *you*."

"I would never. I am in love with Luke. In comparison, Ricky is a walking lump of a ham sandwich."

"You take that back. He's amazing," Heather seethed. "Say it."

"I'd rather die."

Heather held up the lighter to Salem. "Say it, or we're all going up in flames."

"Fine. Ricky is amazing."

"I knew it," Heather sobbed. "I knew you were in love with him."

"Heather, please, sweetie," the chief begged plaintively, "just stop this. No one has to know it was you. If you put down the lighter and give Salem back to Lilith, we can all go home. I won't call the police. You're my daughter."

"Is that why you stole my cat?" I demanded.

"I didn't," the chief insisted. "Salem followed me up here after I pulled that piece of holly out of his paw pad. I saw Heather going to city hall."

"Should have watched the rest of the video, I guess," Luke muttered.

"I was arguing with Heather in my office. I looked down, and there was Salem. Then Heather grabbed him."

"Ugh, why couldn't my birth father be someone rich and handsome, not some overweight fire chief?" Heather asked, lip curled.

The chief looked crushed. "But I've always wanted a daughter."

"I'm sure you two can rekindle your relationship in prison," I said.

"Shut up, Lilith. I'm not going to prison. You're going to prison," Heather said, baring her teeth.

"What? No, I'm not."

"Yes, you are. This whole place is going to burn down, including you, that sad idiot, and your dumb, low-class boyfriend."

"He's not low-class. He's a wonderful man, and any woman would be lucky to have him."

"Not me. I have standards." Heather tossed her hair. "Now, go stand over there with them."

"If you're going to burn this place down, do it," I said to her, walking slowly toward Luke. "Send us all to hell and put us out of this Christmas-induced misery."

"I don't want to burn alive, Lilith! What the fuck!" Luke cried.

"You can shit or get off the pot," I challenged Heather. "There are so many gas fumes in here that this place will go up like a bomb the second you strike the lighter. None of us is making it out of here alive."

The other woman hesitated, her hand on the lighter.

"Heather, please just put the cat down, and we can figure this out. They like me at the police department. I'm sure I can cut you a deal," the chief begged.

"Shut up, old man!" Heather shrieked.

I'd had enough of Heather. So I did what I'd wanted to do since she and Patty had first cut off one of my braids all the way back in first grade. I hefted the ceramic coffee cup and chucked it at Heather's head.

It hit her just below her ear. She stumbled and sank down to the ground, dropping the lighter. Salem struggled out of her grasp, and Heather screamed as the black cat sliced up her face with his sharp claws. "Get it off! Get it off!"

Instead, she was tackled by Luke. "Get the lighter!"

I scooped it up while Luke held Heather down with his knee.

"My poor baby," Chief Reynolds sobbed.

"I can't believe I'm related to her," Luke muttered.

"Hands up! Police!"

Bobby and Winston stormed in with the rest of the force.

"Ugh, it stinks in here," Winston complained.

"Arrest this woman for the murder of Patty Harrison." I pointed at Heather.

"No fair," Bobby complained as he took out his handcuffs. "We were supposed to solve the murder."

Svensson PharmaTech sent down its hazmat team to clean up the gasoline. Several workers in white hazmat suits set up a cleaning station on the sidewalk in front of city hall.

I helped Luke strip out of his clothes, then the hazmat team used special soap and solvent agents to clean the gas off him. The contaminated water was put into tanks to be disposed of properly, not sent down the storm drains.

"Salem, they're trying to help," I told the cat as he meowed pitifully in the plastic bucket at Luke's feet.

Salem wailed louder, and a dog barked.

"Smokey's mad he missed the fun," Cliff joked, pulling back the curtain.

"Dude!"

There was a crowd of drunk onlookers because it was the Christmas market at nine p.m. and what else were you going to do except drink elf-tinis and watch the capture of a murderer? Front-row seats were a hot-ticket item. Well, not as hot as Luke.

There were wolf whistles and applause as the women in the crowd were treated to a glimpse of Luke's broad, muscled chest. Then I pulled the curtain closed.

"Sorry, man," Cliff called.

"Officer! Officer!" Penny, wearing a red jacket and earmuffs, appeared and puffed up. "I'm here to report the murderer has been found."

"Another one?" Officer Girthman asked.

Penny pulled out the buckle. "We have evidence. My friend was attacked, and her cat was catnapped."

"Penny..." I sighed.

"No. I got this, Lilith. I also found the adoption records providing motive. It was the chief! Anna's his daughter. He killed Patty to get back at her for how she treated Anna."

"Actually, Heather killed Patty."

Penny steamrolled on. "The buckle, therefore, must belong to him. Arrest this man!" She pointed at the chief, who was just finishing up with his own ice-cold detox shower.

"Penny! No, Heather is the one who killed Patty because she was in love with Ricky and thought Ricky ended their affair to go back to Patty when really he went to Ashley."

"Really?" Penny sat down on a bench. "But Heather was trying to name a holiday in Patty's honor."

I took the buckle from her.

"I don't want a holiday in her honor! I hate that bitch!" Heather screeched as the police hauled her away in handcuffs.

"Oh my god, you killed Patty?" Ashley cried from the crowd.

"You skank. You home-wrecker!" Heather tried to break away from the police to attack Ashley, but they stuffed her into a squad car.

David appeared out of the crowd, racing after it as it drove away. "I love you, Heather! I'm going to pay your bail and visit you in prison."

"You think you know someone," Morticia said, loping up. "I can't believe you didn't let me come help you. Now Salem's covered in gasoline, and you apparently have a boyfriend."

"She's going to be my wife," Luke interjected.

"It's so romantic how you two met." Penny swooned.

"Wait," the chief said, confused. "Did I hear you say that Heather isn't my daughter?"

CHAPTER 30
Luke

After the big arrest, the Svensson PharmaTech hazmat team cordoned off the area and didn't let anyone near city hall while they cleaned up the gasoline spilled in the clock tower.

The town retired to Anna's café. The chief and Anna were hugging and crying by the counter as she served drinks.

I brought over tea for Lilith. Her sister and Penny were talking with several other residents about Heather's identity as the murderer and the abduction of Salem the cat, who was the star of the show.

"Spinach puff?" I slid the plate over to Lilith on the small café table.

"Starving," she said, grabbing it, and took a bite. "Oh!" She wiped her mouth then dug into her pocket and held out a metal buckle. "I believe this is yours."

"Thanks for finding it," I said, taking the buckle from her. "Guess you didn't find the strap."

"A strap?"

I rubbed my thumb over the worn buckle.

"Was that your dad's?" Lilith asked carefully.

I barked out a laugh. "That asshole? No, just a random firefighter who came to my school in first grade the week before Christmas to talk about fireplace safety. You know, keeping it clean, making sure the logs are stable." I smiled at the memory. "I thought he was the coolest thing ever, and that's what I wanted to be when I grew up. A real live hero. He gave me a strap on a buckle that said Queens Fire Department Station 124. It was my good-luck charm." I leaned over to kiss her. "Guess it worked, since I met you."

***

"You know," I said to Lilith in the dark bedroom after I'd shown her just how much I loved her, "I'm continuing the tradition of going to schools to teach fire safety. I could use a demonstration helper, if you're interested."

Lilith wrapped her arms around my neck and kissed me soundly. "Like I said, I'm all yours this Christmas, since I have no stall and no wares."

I rubbed her bare back. "I am sorry about your stall."

She sighed. "Christmas was never my holiday, though with you, I think I might have a merry Christmas."

"I love you, Lilith. And I heard you say you love me, and you can't take it back."

"Fine. I love you."

"I want to be with you for all your Christmases and Halloweens," I swore.

"Are you sure? You literally just met me."

"And yet I've saved your life twice."

"Not to toot your own horn, of course." She slid her hand down to my Christmas package, making me hiss.

"I love you," I said. "Does it have to be that deep? That's why I like Christmas. It's pure and uncomplicated."

"On the contrary, Christmas is very complicated," she said, resting her chin on my chest. "That's why I like Halloween. It's just candy and spookiness—no family drama."

CHAPTER 31

"**S**he was lying on the ground just like that." Luke's voice sounded like Darth Vader's through the firefighter mask he wore. "In a fire situation, if someone is unconscious, I don't pick them up like in the movies, where you carry them like a baby, because if she's unconscious, she's just going to fall out of my arms like a noodle."

The class of kids laughed as I mimed being a noodle.

"I'll raise her up to a standing position, flip her over my back, then carry her out." He carried me around the room to applause from the kids and a swoon from their teacher. I thought it was more directed at him because I was not in a comfortable or attractive position.

Luke easily set me down then pulled off his mask.

"What do we do in case of a fire? Get out and stay out," he chorused with the class. "Don't be like Lilith and run back in for a pet."

"Don't be like Lilith," the class of first graders repeated solemnly.

"I will find your pets. I promise," Luke said. "Now, I think Smokey has some fridge magnets for everyone."

Tail wagging, the dog carried around a bag filled with magnets and key chains for the kids. They took the swag then ran over to touch Luke's uniform. He bent down while the kids pulled at the buckles, tried on the hat and mask, and felt how heavy the oxygen tank he wore was.

The scene was literally the cutest thing I'd ever seen and made me want to put up a Christmas tree, bake cookies, and birth as many babies as I could.

"Girl, I think I'm pregnant just looking at him," the teacher joked.

***

"Thank you so much for coming by," the principal gushed to Luke after we'd made the rounds of all the first-grade classrooms.

"I had a great helper. Two great helpers," he said as Smokey wagged his tail. "And now we're going to one of my favorite events besides holiday parties—a baby shower!"

"I feel like you're more excited about my niece than I am," I said as we headed out to the parking lot.

"I told you I love babies." He grabbed me around the waist, picked me up, and threw me over his shoulder.

***

Morticia had insisted on city hall's clock tower as the baby shower venue. The hazmat team had declared it clean the week after Heather's arrest, and Penny and I had decorated it in a *Nightmare Before Christmas* theme.

A Christmas tree with ornaments crafted to look like the Claymation characters from the movie decorated one corner. Tables were adorned with centerpieces featuring miniature versions of Jack and Sally nestled among baby onesies, plush toys, and tiny baby bottles. Black roses and glowing candles added an eerie holiday touch.

Yeah, I had a lot of time on my hands.

My twin with her husband, Jonathan, both stood next to a metal chair featuring elf gremlins that I'd custom-made, surrounded by all their presents. Morticia was wearing a lacy-collared black dress that showed off her baby bump.

"Congratulations!" Ada hugged her then set down a gift bag of Christmas baby swag. "When are you due, Lilith?" she asked.

"She's not married yet," the fire chief joked.

"Don't wait for marriage," Ada whispered to me. "You're old, and your eggs are shriveling up and dying as we speak. Merry Christmas. I made English toffee."

"I love living in a small town," I said.

Penny giggled.

"This is a great baby shower," Luke said, handing me a cup of black-cherry holiday punch, my own recipe. "I had them put booze in yours."

"This is supposed to be a dry baby shower." I accepted the glass.

"There are several senior citizens in attendance who will make it boozy if you show them your abs."

I hesitated then said, "I made you a solstice gift. But I'm giving it to you early in case you hate it."

"Did you make it with love and holiday cheer?" he joked.

"Love, yes. Holiday cheer… eh?"

My boyfriend removed the top off the small black box, then his face lit up.

"I know it's not the same strap you had. I'm still trying to find one."

"I love it." He kissed me. "It's perfect."

"It's a little Christmas, a little bit Halloween."

Luke held it up. "Look, it's the elves burning down the North Pole."

"Santa hadn't been paying them. The checks start bouncing. The elves got mad."

"I didn't know you knew embroidery."

"I have many secrets." I waggled my fingers at his face.

Luke grabbed my hand and kissed the tips of my fingers.

Morticia suddenly banged her spoon on her glass and pointed at Luke.

"I know this is Morticia's baby shower," Luke said, climbing up on a crate. "But this was her idea."

My sister raised her glass to me.

Luke addressed the crowd. "Lilith has traditionally not been a fan of Christmas, and if they'd all gone like this one has, I couldn't blame her. Almost killed several times, stall burned down, and accused of being a murderer. I know the Christmas season is almost over, but Harrogate does have the Valentine's Day Market, so I think you can stretch this out."

"Stretch what out?" I asked.

"Lilith, Uncle Don and I have been working to make you a new stall, bigger and cooler than the last one!" Luke said.

"I've seen it, and I'm authorizing you to keep your cat and sell as many cookies as you want," Ada interjected, sweeping me into a bone-crushing hug. "You better get on those babies. No excuses."

Morticia hugged me next. "You're going to be an amazing aunt. I couldn't ask for a more wonderful sister."

"Let's go see it," Penny demanded, ushering everyone to the stairs.

An Airstream was parked in front of city hall on Main Street. Sleek and silver, it had a sign that read Enter if You Dare!

"I can't believe you did all this!" I turned to Luke. "I love you."

"I love and adore and worship you." He had that dopey smile on his face.

I opened the door of the trailer to see Salem waiting on the wood countertop. The cat meowed a greeting at me.

"He's holding down the fort," Luke joked.

"Oh my gosh!" Several teenage girls raced up, phones out. "We love your new stall."

"Do you have more spider cookies in?"

"We need them for a video."

"Well, I—"

"Yes, she does." Morticia smiled at me. "In the cookie case."

"A cookie case?" I asked.

"Maybe you should go inside and check out your new stall," Penny said giddily.

The inside of the Airstream had been fitted with reclaimed wood with dark, ornate accents. The ceiling and walls were a dark charcoal. A tea kettle whistled on a small wood stove, and the back of the trailer held a small dressing room with a black-velvet curtain. Wood shelves held a sampling of my merchandise. Front and center was a glass-encased cookie counter.

"Do you do Christmas tree ornaments?" one girl asked as I rang up her cookie purchase.

"Not yet," Luke said, leaning in the doorway.

Another girl shot me a thumbs-up on her way out.

Luke swept me into his arms, kissing me. His head almost grazed the top of the trailer.

"We're going to have to be careful when we try to make a baby in here," I deadpanned.

His mouth dropped open.

"What? I have to top this Christmas present somehow, right?"

EPILOGUE

One year later...

O ne year later...
The door to the rambling Victorian home creaked open. In the attic, the bats stirred, and a black cat sitting in front of the fire hissed.

A spooky, cozy autumn scene?

Not a chance.

The cat was wearing a custom-knitted holiday sweater.

A Dalmatian burst through the door, careening into the living room.

"You better not knock down my snacks," I warned the dog, who wagged his tail and rubbed his large body all over my black dress, getting white hairs everywhere.

Luke came in carrying the Christmas tree. Well, *a* tree. We had multiple trees.

"Another one?" I asked him as he set it down in a waiting Christmas tree stand.

"We are hosting, Lilith," he told me, sweeping me into his arms, then he twirled me around and kissed me until I was dizzy.

"I don't think we have enough ornaments," I said breathlessly.

"Put some spiderwebs on it and call it a day." Luke shrugged.

"That doesn't fit with the Victorian Christmas aesthetic."

Luke grinned. "It's a little bit of you, a little bit of me."

"You went all out with me on Halloween," I reminded him. "You were really in character as Igor."

"I love holidays," he said, giving me that infectious smile with the dimple and everything. He was as sappy as a Hallmark Christmas card, but I loved him so much anyway.

Luke followed me into the spacious kitchen of the historic Victorian home. Turned out you could sell a lot of cookies after going viral on social media. Enough to buy your dream home.

To be fair, we got it for a steal because the former owner was an elderly resident whose family had been in Harrogate for generations, and she was not selling to any newcomers. Not that any newcomers were going to want a ramshackle house that had its last renovation in 1945.

The timer beeped. The animals came racing as I opened up the oven and pulled out a roast goose. Luke was ready with tongs and a fork to transfer the bird to a platter.

"I'll take the old bird out," Luke said, carrying the platter into the living room.

"Put some foil on it," I called.

Then I put the finishing touches on the spread. The long dining-room table that Luke and the chief had built from scrap wood in the back was covered with red-and-green runners, glowing candles, and bunches of garland.

At one end, I had the desserts—carefully decorated cakes, an array of pies, and an assortment of cookies, including spider cookies because I wasn't going to completely give in to Christmas sweetness. The other end held appetizers like stuffed mushrooms, cranberry brie bites, shrimp cocktails, and spinach puffs.

In the middle of the table were the entrees—garlic-and-cheese mashed potatoes, ham, a huge turkey Luke had brought back, lobster mac 'n' cheese, clam pasta for people who didn't want to eat meat, bacon-wrapped green beans, homemade rolls with herb butter, butternut squash risotto, a prime-rib roast, roasted brussels sprouts, potato gratin, and of course, three kinds of stuffing.

And I had been afraid I was going to run out of food.

You couldn't have a holiday party and not invite half the town. You'd be hearing about it until next Christmas.

Luke crossed his arms and regarded the spread. "It's almost scary how well you're able to do the traditional Christmas housewife stuff. I'm half expecting a newt to pop out of that Yule log. Also, is that a cauldron?"

"Of Christmas punch."

"Is there something swimming in it?" He frowned.

"Canapé?" I held out a tray to him.

I was wearing fifties-housewife garb. Well, the goth version. A black dress was Christmassy as long as it was paired with red lipstick, right?

The doorbell rang.

"Merry Christmas!" my sister called. She had a big smile on her face.

Salem ran under the couch and hissed at her. I resisted the urge to pull out my pepper spray.

Morticia's face dropped back to her neutral death-mask expression.

"Sister," I greeted her, leaning in to air-kiss her cheeks.

"Yes, I know. I'll never do that again. I was attempting to get into the holiday spirit."

"I told her the smile was creepier than anything you'd see during Halloween," Jonathan said happily. There was a man who loved Christmas as much as Luke did.

My boyfriend immediately went over to him to coo over the little baby strapped to his chest.

"I'm starving," Morticia declared.

"I made you special tea for nursing mothers."

"I think she'd rather have some of those bacon-wrapped green beans," Jonathan joked.

"Ooh," Penny called from the door, "did I just hear you trying to pawn off that nasty-ass tea on poor Morticia?"

Penny's husband, Garrett, prowled in after her, followed by the rest of his dozens of brothers and their wives and girlfriends.

"I believe you didn't make enough food, Lilith," Morticia stated.

"This house has two kitchens, and I have another packed with food," I informed her. "No one will starve."

"Except for these poor animals," Jonathan said, wrestling with the big Dalmatian on the floor while Luke cradled my niece.

"You're going to get your suit dirty," his older brother chastised him.

Yeah, my in-law brought all his family. The house was packed, and none of the townspeople had shown up yet.

"We might need to take this holiday party out into the yard," Luke said to me.

"I have more turkeys to deep-fry if things become dicey," I said out of the side of my mouth.

The doorbell rang and rang as more people arrived, shouting, "Merry Christmas!"

Finally, Penny told Garrett's little brothers to man the door and take coats and hats. Several more were instructed to pass out drinks and help elderly residents get food.

The fire chief and Anna arrived while the little boys were sorting out where to put the coats.

Anna hugged me then handed me a casserole. "I have five more in the car."

When the party was in full swing, Luke jumped onto a table and clinked his glass.

"We just want to thank everyone for coming to the inaugural holiday party at the Reynolds-DiRizzio house! Because it's the holidays and all our friends and family are here, I just want to take a moment to say how glad I am to have moved to Harrogate and found Lilith. This is the best Christmas ever, and I know there are many more to come. And to make sure of that…"

He jumped off the table, bent down on one knee in front of me, and pulled a black box out of his pocket.

"Lilith," he said, opening it. "From the moment I met you, your strength, your uniqueness, and your incredible heart were more captivating than any flame. Also, those cookies were a big draw. I can't imagine loving anyone as much as I love you. You make every day feel like Christmas. Will you do me the honor of marrying me? Hopefully on Christmas, but I'll take Halloween."

"Yes," I said, looking down at him, not sure why the room seemed shimmery. Must have been magic because I definitely was not crying. "I love you, and you make every day feel like the perfect autumn day. I'd love nothing more than to spend the rest of my life with you."

My fiancé slipped the black diamond onto my finger then stood up to cheers and pops of champagne. He swept me into his strong arms and kissed me like he couldn't believe I was his.

"Speech, speech!" several people cried.

I hopped onto the table.

"This is the best Christmas present ever," I said, "but I do have one quibble. You see, I had the perfect present planned for this evening, and Luke stole my thunder."

Luke gave me a questioning look. I smirked.

"Luke, we're having a baby."

"Yes!" Luke fell to his knees and pumped his fists. Then he grabbed my waist and kissed my belly. "Your mom makes amazing cookies," he whispered to the waistband.

"We're naming her Wednesday," Luke declared.

"I thought we would name her, like, Hope or something Christmassy," I argued.

"I want another holiday goth just like you," Luke said stubbornly.

"You could do both." Morticia held up her empty teacup to show me the leaves. "Twins. Merry Christmas!"

Luke kissed me. "Best present ever!"

ACKNOWLEDGEMENTS

A big thank you to Red Adept Editing for editing and proofreading.

And finally a big thank you to all the readers! I had a great time writing this hilarious book! Please try not to choke on your wine while reading!!!

About the Author

If you like steamy romantic comedy novels with a creative streak, then I'm your girl!

Architect by day, writer by night, I love matcha green tea, chocolate, and books! So many books...

Sign up for my mailing list to get special bonus content, free books, giveaways, and more!

http://alinajacobs.com/mailinglist.html

Made in United States
Orlando, FL
02 November 2024

53365511R00120